NEVER A DULL MOMENT:

THE NICK JR. STORY

D I A N A   C A R T E R

Let's Do This Publishing

Never a Dull Moment: The Nick Jr. Story

Mystery/Family Drama

All Rights Reserved

Copyright © 2018 by Diana Carter

LET'S DO THIS PUBLISHING, LLC
P.O. Box 300795
Drayton Plaines, MI 48330

ISBN 13: 978-0-9997106-5-4

Cover Designed by Professional Instant Printing. All Rights Reserved

PRINTED IN THE UNITED STATES OF AMERICA

OTHER BOOKS WRITTEN BY DIANA CARTER

BROKEN PROMISES SERIES

Book 1	Book 2	Book 3	Spin-Off

Dark Revenge:
The Trey Taylor Story

THE SISTER FACTOR SERIES

Book 1	Book 2	Book 3	Book 4

Dedication

Thanking God for the many blessings He has brought into my life is a pleasurable duty for me to perform each day. I couldn't imagine a life without Him in it. When going through trials and tribulations, I sometimes feel alone, until I realize I'm never alone when I put Him first in my life. This book is a special dedication to a person that recently came into my life that I consider a friend, mentor, and an awesome God loving person, Darliss Bachelor. Darliss has mentored and shaped my life in ways that is hard to explain. May God continue to bless her with good health, and the kind spirit she shares with so many people.

Acknowledgements

I have recently taken a step back to reevaluate my life and the direction in which it is going. I never thought I would get this far in a career I have become so passionate about. This title *Never a Dull Moment: The Nick Jr. Story* is the Spin-off to the four-book *The Sister Factor* series. After completing this series I felt it wasn't totally complete, because Junior didn't have his story.

I would like to take the time out to thank a number of people, beginning with the great team I call my work family: Matt Bouvier, Bob Clancy, Bethany Schultz, Glenda Cruz, Melissa Kelly, Emily Marsden, and Tracy Nadeau. You guys have been such a pleasure to work with over the last two years. I look forward to coming to work every day because I get to work with such an awesome group of people. Also, part of my work family, a big shout out to: Catherine McFarland, Donna Niezgoda, Lisa Viazanko, and Shannon Meek. You guys are special to me.

Next, I would like to thank, Sue Tolder. Although I only worked with her for a short time, I came to know her as a kindhearted and genuine person. Stay strong with God's blessings. I can't leave out

Tem Harris. Tem has not only been my hair stylist for more than thirty years, but a true friend. She has been a sounding board when I was sometimes at my wits end. Thank you so much for being there for me in my many times of need.

Lastly, I would like to thank my dear family and friends that have supported me over the years when I felt like giving up. Writing and getting your work published is a time consuming task. The few times when I had writers block or just didn't feel like finishing a book I started, I think about the people that have supported me throughout my career and knew it would be unfair to them for me to give up. So, as I put this title to rest and start the next one, I want to say thank you, thank you, thank you to all of you from the bottom of my heart.

God's blessings,

Diana Carter

Chapter One

The Morgan family sat in the emergency rooms waiting to get an update on Alyssa and Annika. It had been a long night. The family was divided because some of them were with Annika (Nika), Junior and Alyssa's six-month old daughter. Junior felt guilty that he couldn't be in two places at once, so he divided his time between his wife and daughter.

Junior thought he would never find a woman he loved more than Jalissa (his first wife), but it was love at first sight when he met Alyssa. His sisters and dad were upset when he took an interest in Alyssa because it was during the time that Alyssa was investigating, Krystal his baby sister. He didn't see anything wrong with what he was doing and told his family Alyssa was just doing her job. Their courtship was short and sweet and it almost had Junior relocating to New York. Alyssa worked for the FBI as an agent assigned to investigate a drug crime lord.

That was more than two years ago and so much had happened since. Krystal was found innocent of the part she played in the drug ring, even though she was more involved than she let her family believed. Diamond, the oldest of Junior's four sisters was an attorney that defended Krystal, even though she had almost lost her life in the process. The second oldest sister, Dior life had finally calmed down after going through some rocky times with an interfering sister-in-law and ex-girlfriend. Now she and her husband Charlie were the proud parents of CJ (Charlie's son with ex-girlfriend) and Charlotte (Char) their two-year old daughter. Dior and Charlie now have full custody of CJ after the unexpected death of CJ's mom, Carmen. Before Junior could continue to explore his thoughts a drained doctor and nurse approached him.

"Mr. Morgan, we have your wife stabilized for the time being. She suffered internal injuries and lots of bruising."

"When can I see her, doctor?"

"Not for a few hours. She is in recovery right now. A nurse will be out to get you once we have her settled into her room."

"Ok. Thanks, Doc." Junior shook the doctor's hand, "My family would be here since I have to run back and forth between my wife and daughter."

"That's not a problem, Mr. Morgan." The doctor and nurse turned and left the waiting room.

"Junior, you can go check on Nika. We can stay and let you know when it's time to see Alyssa." Kristina, Junior's second youngest sister said.

"Thanks, Kristy. I think I will join the others to check on the baby. When Joe gets here please send him to the nursery." Junior left his sisters and brothers-in-laws to meet with his dad, step-mom, and auntie who were waiting on an update on the baby.

Before Junior headed to the nursery he went to a secluded area in the hospital and had a cry. How his life could have changed so much in the last few months. It started off with the video that was sent to him of Alyssa and her former partner in the drug case, Kane Karter having sex. Alyssa tried to explain to him that was an old video because she hadn't had a sexual relationship with Kane for over three years. Junior's problem was that he didn't know they had a relationship at all. This took him back to the time when he found out Jalissa had cheated on him. Even though he tried to be reasonable about it since the relationship happened before they even knew each other, he found it hard to get it out of his mind.

Things had gotten bad between them and that is why he didn't know that his wife and daughter were in trouble. Junior thanked God that their daughter barely suffered at all thanks to Alyssa's quick thinking, but she didn't fare as well as Annika. Alyssa was thrown from the moving car that she and Annika were in when the accident happened.

Junior knew it was time to dry his tears and go see his baby girl. When he arrived at the nursey his step-mom had a big smile on her face explaining the baby was checked out and would be discharged soon.

"Thank God. They won't let me see Alyssa until she is moved into a room, but the doctor said she came through the surgery just fine." Junior went to sit by his, Auntie Denise (his dad's younger sister).

"How are you holding up, Son?" Nick, Junior's dad asked.

"It still seems like a dream. I wished I had done so many things differently. I know Alyssa isn't Jalissa, but I still treated her like an enemy when that video came out."

"Don't worry about that now. You will have time to make it up to her. We all have a tenancy of flying off the handle and being unreasonable right, Nick?" Bethany directed to her husband since he was so unfair to Dillon and Reggie (Diamond and Kristina's husbands), when Reggie had his mental meltdown a few years ago.

"Don't go there, Beth. That was a long time ago and should not be brought up again." Nick said.

"I agree, with Beth, Nicky. Unfortunately, Junior inherited your inability to see straight when your heart is hurting." Denise added.

"Not you too, Neicy, Junior had a right to feel the way he did. When you are married to someone you are supposed to be upfront about anything that can create misunderstandings."

"No, Dad, I overreacted. With all the drama with Jalissa and the changes in Joe, I wasn't being a good husband to Alyssa." Junior clarified, "I just pray we can get back on track." Before Junior could say anything else, the nurse told him that his daughter was ready to be discharged.

Chapter Two

Junior sat by his wife's bedside waiting on her to wake up. She had been in and out consciousness since she was brought into the hospital. He was glad he didn't have to worry about Annika since she was staying with his dad and step-mom. Joe was another story. He was upset with Junior because he was forced to stay at his maternal grandparents instead of home. Junior didn't want to leave Joe unattended at home because he didn't trust that he would be responsible.

Junior asked his family not to spend too much time at the hospital because the doctors didn't know how long it would be before Alyssa could receive visitors. All of his sisters understood, but Diamond. She felt she should be there since she knew the police would have to question Alyssa once she was up to being interviewed. As Alyssa attorney, Diamond didn't want her to answer any questions unless she was present.

As Junior sat there lost in his thoughts, he went back to the first day he met Alyssa. He was in Diamond's office when Alyssa showed up unannounced. This pissed Diamond off. When Alyssa walked in Junior couldn't believe his eyes. Not only was she the most beautiful woman he had ever seen, but she made him come alive. He had been in the dumps because he couldn't deal with the dating scene now that he and Jalissa were divorced. His reaction pissed Diamond off even further because this was the woman who was fighting to send their baby sister to prison.

The next few times Junior came into contact with Alyssa were even more electrifying. On one of these occasions he happened to be around his other sisters Dior and Kristina. Dior was even more pissed than Diamond that Junior was behaving so insensitive. Dior had always been Krystal's protector while Diamond had always been Kristina's.

The fourth time Junior saw Alyssa, he asked her out. She turned him down flat, but he knew it was because she was still working on the case. He joined the case with Diamond and Dior mainly so he could be close to Alyssa, even though he wanted to help his baby sister. His dad and the rest of the family told him to leave it along, but it was too late for Junior to take their advice. He thought his love for Jalissa was so powerful nothing could compare, but what he felt for Alyssa went beyond words.

Through the safe houses and their close calls with death, Junior's interest in Alyssa never wavered. Once the case was over,

Alyssa finally accepted his date offer. After dating for only one month, Junior announced to his family that he was moving to New York. The move never happened because Alyssa didn't want Junior to uproot Joe so they had a long distant relationship for six months. Alyssa decided to take time off from work and moved to Atlanta to be with Junior and Joe.

The following year in July, Junior and Alyssa were married. Things had been moving along good for them even though Joe started acting out. Junior didn't understand the reason behind Joe's behavior change, so this concerned him. He wondered if it was the baby, but when he asked Joe all he would say is he was glad to be a big brother. Junior didn't think it was Alyssa because she and Joe had a good relationship.

Junior went back to a conversation he had with Alyssa where she suggested that Junior should talk to Joe about drugs.

"Junior, I don't want to alarm you baby, but do you think that Joe's behavioral change has to do with drugs?"

"What are you suggesting, Lyssa, that Joe is doing drugs?" *Junior asked.*

"I'm not suggesting anything. I just asked because I ran across a case one time where the teen had started using drugs without his parents' knowledge." Alyssa explained, cringing every time Junior called her Lyssa.

"That's doesn't mean that Joe is using. I know he is facing many challenges in his life with his mom running in and out of his life, but he is not stupid enough to use drugs."

"Junior, it's not just his mom's actions he has to deal with, but also me, the baby, and dealing with peer pressure."

"Joe IS NOT using drugs. I don't want to talk about this again."

Junior remembered storming out the door without giving Alyssa a chance to say anything else. Looking at his wife now, Junior realized the many times he was unfair to her and vowed to make it up to her as soon as possible.

Later that afternoon Nick and Bethany sat in their family room discussing Junior. Nick didn't like when he and wife wasn't in agreement. He didn't understand how Bethany couldn't see that Alyssa actions made Junior react negatively to what had happened over the last few months. They talked about this several times without coming to an agreement. He realized his wife could be just as stubborn as he at times. He was glad when Diamond finally arrived.

"No matter how I try to get along with that man, he gets on my nerves faster than anyone, I know." Diamond said even before she greeted her parents. They knew she was talking about Lance (Dior's husband, Charlie best friend).

"Calm down, Di. What's going on with Lance?" Nick asked.

"Well, I just came back from a meeting with him and he is as tight lipped as ever. He knew I was there on Alyssa's behalf. I wanted to be able to give Junior some good news when I went to the hospital later."

"Di, you're going to have to stop butting heads with Lance. It doesn't have to be a tug-a-war every time you guys are involved in the same case." Bethany said to her stubborn daughter.

"Mom, you don't understand. That man goes out of his way to try to make me beg for information I'm entitle to."

"Di, your, Mom is right. I think you enjoy giving him a hard time. He has mellowed a lot over the years since, Dior's case." Nick added.

"Okay, for Dior's sake I'll try to ignore his crappy attitude. Now let's talk about my big brother. What's going on with him, Dad?"

"Di, your, Mom and I were just talking about that. Junior is all over the place because he lives in constant fear of losing Alyssa. He's not confident that she loves him enough to get through rough times in their marriage."

"We'll, he needs to get over himself. How much is she going to have to prove for him to chill? I mean the lady gave up her career and moved to a different state just to be with him." Diamond said.

"Di, let's agree to disagree. I hope there isn't anything else going on with Alyssa. The facts just not adding up." Nick said.

"I'm going to leave you two to talk shop. If you need me honey, I will be in my office." Bethany gave Nick and Diamond a brief hug before she left the room.

"Ok, Dad. Let's get down to business." Diamond said.

"Good idea, Di." Nick said, as he and Diamond worked for a few hours before she headed out to meet Junior at the hospital.

Chapter Three

A few days after meeting with her dad, Diamond sat with Kristina in Alyssa's room talking quietly. It was hard, but they finally convinced Junior to go home and get some rest and spend time with Joe and Annika. Alyssa regained consciousness occasionally, but not for long. Kristina wanted to talk to Diamond privately so she asked her to take a walk with her. She was a big believer that an unconscious person can hear everything that goes on around them. Once they were inside Diamond's car, Kristina started the conversation.

"Di, I think it's a lot more going on with Alyssa than what she is letting Junior know."

"I'm getting the same feeling. I know she loves our brother, but I think something from her past has come back to haunt her. It was too easy for her to give up her career and life in New York." Diamond said, even though she defended Alyssa to her parents.

"Junior is headed for heartache. I just hope it is not on the level of what he experienced with Jalissa."

"I know. It doesn't help that dad is telling Junior that he has a right to be angry and disappointed in his wife. I think it has him and mom at odds too." Diamond added.

"Dad is restless. He needs to find something to do besides work mom's nerves. When he finally retired and let you take over, I don't think he realized how different his life would become." Kristina said rubbing her face.

"Kristy, that is why I do my best to keep him updated on what is happening at the firm. Some of the changes I implemented I think he's okay with, but I get the feeling that he doesn't like all of my changes."

"What do you think will happen when Krystal gets back home? She still isn't giving Alyssa a chance to bond with her. I know she loves Nika, but if she could stay close to her without getting involved with Alyssa, she would do it in a heartbeat."

"Krystal needs to chill. She is the last person that has room to judge. After all she put this family through, she needs to get over herself. I'm just glad Dillon finally forgiven her."

"I guess we better get back in there. If Junior finds out we left Alyssa alone, he would have a fit." Kristina said.

"You're right about that, Kristy, but we won't stay much longer because you need your rest too." Diamond and Kristina returned to

Alyssa's room. Kristina was four months pregnant with the son her husband wanted so badly.

It was almost three o'clock in the afternoon when Junior woke up and got dress. He heard Joe downstairs, so he thought it was the perfect time to talk to him since the baby was still at his dad and step-mom's. Joe had been distant lately. Junior noticed that he has been talking to his mom more often. Jalissa was now settled in her new life in Boston and had even remarried. When she came to visit Joe, and her parents, she seemed more at peace. She had even stop being so hateful towards Junior.

Heading downstairs Junior didn't know what to expect from Joe. His demeanor was so hot and cold it was hard for Junior to keep up with his mood swings. As Junior headed to the family room, he became upset when he found Joe in there eating and watching one of his favorite programs. Junior had told Joe more than once not to eat anywhere in the house outside of the kitchen and dining rooms. That was the rule when his mom was alive, so Junior wanted to still respect her wishes.

"Hey, Joe, didn't we have a talk about where you are supposed to eat?" Junior asked.

"I forgot." That was all Joe said and continued to eat and watch his program.

"Joe, please turn that off so we can talk."

"Dad, can we talk later? I had a hard day at school."

"That is partly what I want to talk to you about." Junior said.

"Don't tell me. That weird, Mr. Bob called you."

"Yes, I received a call from him and also from your math teacher. Not to mention the letters that are still coming in regarding your attendance."

"Dad, what more do you want from me? I have brought all of my grades up and been following your strict rules around here."

"Joe, I want you to talk to me about what is bothering you. Don't tell me nothing, because your behavior has been up and down for over a year now. You only have a few months left in high school and you still haven't selected a college."

"I'm trying, Dad."

"Joe, I know something is wrong. Is it your mom?"

"No, Dad. She finally satisfied that I talk to her every once in a while."

"Son, I don't want to pressure you, but you have got to let me know what's going on. How am I supposed to help you if I don't know what you need help with?"

"Dad, there is nothing wrong. You're starting to sound like Grandma and Grandpa Jones."

"Joe, your grandparents loves you. They're just trying to make sure you are doing okay."

"Well, all they do is nag. That's why I don't like going over there anymore. I wish Nana was still alive." Tears formed in Joe's eyes. "Nothing seems right anymore."

"Joe, I miss, Ma too, but she has been gone for a long time, so you need to find a way to deal with that. I told you, we can go into counseling."

"I'm not crazy, Dad." Joe shouted and ran out of the room."

Junior watched as Joe left his food behind. He guessed his next step was to talk to Kristina. He would see if she would take Joe on as a patient.

Chapter Four

Alyssa was finally awake. She looked around the room and wondered where she was at. Her head hurt badly, but she caught a glimpse of her husband sitting next to her bed nodding. She tried to clear her throat, but it felt like she had swallowed rocks. She moved a little and all she could do was moan because her entire body was hurting. Junior jumped when he heard her moaning and took her hand.

"Hi, sweetie, welcome back. I'll let the nurse know you are awake."

Alyssa squeezed Junior's hand tight to let him know she didn't want him to leave the room. Instead he pushed the signal button next to her bed. A short and stubby lady with a pleasant smile on her faced came into the room and asked Junior to give her room so she could take Alyssa vitals.

"Nurse, why does she look so scared?" Junior asked.

"She is probably just trying to get adjusted to her surroundings." The nurse said. The doctor came into the room and asked Junior to leave for a few minutes. Junior went over to Alyssa, kissed her forehead and told her he would be right outside.

Junior was so happy he didn't know who to call first. After his disturbing talk with Joe early he had a lot on his mind. Junior called his Dad and asked him to let the rest of the family know that Alyssa was awake. After hanging up from his dad, Junior called Joe on his cell and on the landline at home, but didn't get an answer. He told Joe before he left home not to leave the house. He didn't know if Joe listened and was just ignoring his calls or what. He decided to text Joe and asked him to call him immediately. He didn't want to leave the good news about Alyssa on a voice mail or text.

While he was waiting for the doctor to finish Alyssa's examine, Junior tried to think back when he first noticed Joe's behavioral change. His mom had passed away a little over three years ago. Joe had gotten very close to Melissa and was having a hard time when they told him about her cancer. Melissa died a few weeks after letting her family know about her condition.

Joe seemed to get over his sadness after a few months passed. But then he started to become withdrawn. Junior put that down to his and Jalissa fight for custody over him. Junior started noticing that Joe was staying in his room more often and stop associating with his friends. When Junior became involved with Alyssa months later Joe seemed to return to his normal self. He was spending time with his friends and Jalissa's parents. He and Alyssa hit it off just as quickly as Junior and Alyssa did.

Junior was happy because he wanted Joe to be as happy as he was with Alyssa's becoming part of their family. He knew Alyssa's age was a factor. She was able to get them involved into activities that a teenager would enjoy. As Junior was sitting there thinking about Joe's change it was when they told him about Alyssa's pregnancy. Joe said he was okay, but now that Junior was thinking about it this seemed like the beginning of Joe's problems. When a hand pressed lightly on his shoulder, Junior was startled.

"Man, you didn't hear me talking to you?" Dillon asked. He and Reggie was standing in front of Junior with strange looks on their faces.

"Sorry, I was just thinking about Joe. The doctor is checking on Alyssa."

"We know. The ladies couldn't get away so we were nominated to come keep you company." Reggie said.

"Thanks guys, but that wasn't necessary. I know both of you have better things to do then to hang out in this dreary place."

"We're cool. I figure we could talk you into going out for a bit. We haven't gotten away in a little while. We have Charlie and Lance on standby." Dillon said.

"I don't think I should leave, Alyssa. She looked scared to death when she regained consciousness."

"We can slip away after you see her for a few hours. It will be good for you to have time away from everything." Dillion persisted.

"Okay. I tell you what. I will meet you guys in about an hour at the lounge. I am kind of going stir crazy here. Dad and Mama Beth told me, I better not show back at their house until I get some rest." Junior told the fellas he would see them shortly and went into the room to check on his wife.

Kristina had her hands full. Diamond and Dior was at her house with all their kids. Char was asleep, but the twins, CJ, and Miracle was wide awake giving Marissa a run for her money. They were in the playroom watching a video while the ladies were in the family room enjoying their visit together. Dior started the conversation off by letting her sisters know that Krystal would be back in a few days.

"Don't remind us. We have to be ready to deal with her drama and complaining about Alyssa. I never thought the day would come that she would be protective of Junior." Diamond said.

"That goes to show you, Di, people can change. Just look how Brandy went for icy cold to lukewarm." Dior chimed in.

"You're right, Dior. That was one sister, I would have betted my license on that she would not come around." Kristina added.

"Okay, Kristy, what was your reason for us coming over here? I know part of it was because the men are together." Diamond asked her younger sister.

"I think we need to get in front of this Junior situation. We don't want his marriage to be like what he had with Jalissa." Kristina responded.

"I told, Kristy when she brought this up before that Junior needs to stop tripping. I know Alyssa should have told him more about her past, but he is overreacting." Diamond said rubbing her hand across her face as she explained to Dior.

"Di feels that Junior is acting like Dad and overreacting instead of thinking." Kristina clarified.

"Well, I'm kind of on the fence with this situation," Dior said. "Speaking from past experience, I think Alyssa is running from a situation that is catching up to her."

"When I get a chance to talk to her, I'll try to find out more and if she is running she needs to stop. She is not alone like she was before. The family will stick by her as long as she comes clean. Even Krystal will be there for her, although it may be with an attitude." Diamond said.

Okay, ladies, I think there isn't too much more we can do until Di talks to Alyssa. Let's call it a day and see how things play out." Kristina suggested. She helped Diamond and Dior get the kids together and after walking them all to the door she checked on Miracle then took a nap.

Chapter Five

Junior sat in his bedroom with so much on his mind he didn't know where he should begin to work on his problems. Now that Alyssa was doing much better and was scheduled to be released tomorrow morning barring any complications, he should be on top of the world. It would be so good to have Annika back home too. She was still at his dad and Bethany's house. Junior wanted to spend time with Joe before the girls came back home.

He took the day off from work to take Joe to his first appointment with Kristina. Kristina told Junior she would give it a shot, but he would be better off taking Joe to a therapist. She wasn't sure Joe would open up to her the way he would with an unbiased therapist. Joe insisted if he had to go to a head doctor he wanted it to be his auntie. Junior planned to take Joe to school when he finished his session, then head to the hospital to see Alyssa.

When Junior first approached Kristina with the possibility of her counseling Joe, she turned him down. She felt she was too closed to Joe to be effective. Additionally, she told Junior she didn't want to damage her relationship with him, because her sessions with Joe would be private. She wouldn't be able to give Junior any information unless it was life threatening without Joe's permission. Junior felt a little uncomfortable with that aspect, but knew he needed to do something right away to get to the root of Joe's problems.

Junior thought back to the time when Joe was born. He was twenty-six and had been married to Jalissa less than a year. His relationship was still strained with his parents because his dad thought he was unmotivated and his mom was busy trying to run his life. Neither of his parents was excited about his marriage. He and Jalissa eloped secretly. His mom refused from the beginning to accept his wife or son.

Cutting the umbilical cord when Joe was born was the most exciting and scariest thing Junior had ever experienced. Thinking back to the conversation he and Jalissa had was memorable. Junior couldn't help but smile.

"Oh my God, Jay, our son looks just like you." Junior said.

"He does look a lot like me, but look at that nose. That is all you honey bunch."

"The ears too. How can such a small head hold up such large ears?"

"I'm so glad we already have a name because I'm so exhausted right now, all I want to do is sleep."

"You get some rest baby. I will let the family know about our newest addition."

Junior was interrupted when Joe stuck his head into the room and told his dad he was ready to get his head shrunk.

"Joe, you shouldn't look at this in such a negative way. I just want you to be able to work through your issues." Junior said.

"I'm ready, Dad." Joe walked out and Junior heard the downstairs door slam behind him.

Kristina sat in her office waiting on Junior and Joe. She had to admit that she was a little anxious. She hadn't treated anyone she was close to since her young sister-in-law, Ashley. At that time, she hadn't started her practice yet. Ashley had a long list of issues she was dealing with, the most traumatic was being molested by her uncle. Her dad's younger brother had been molesting Ashley for a long time, but Ashley was never strong enough to let her family know when it first started. The knock on her door brought Kristina out of her daydream.

"Good morning, guys. Junior I have some paperwork for you to complete. Do you have any questions about the policies we talked about?"

"Thanks, Kristy. I don't have any questions at this time.

"Ok. Once you have completed the forms I will make a copy for your records. The first twenty minutes of the session we will talk together. The last forty minutes I will have a one-on-one with Joe. We will go get a snack while you are completing the forms." Kristina explained then she and Joe left her office. Returning, she went to her desk and asked Junior and Joe to have a seat in front of her desk.

"Can you guys tell me what has brought you here today?" Kristina asked.

Since Joe sat there with a grim look on his face, Junior answered the question. "Well, we have been having communication issues at home. I've been worried about Joe because he seems to be cutting himself off from the family."

"Joe, do you have anything to add to what your, Dad said?"

"No, I don't." Joe answered.

"Junior is there anything else you would like to say before you leave?" Kristina asked.

"I just want Joe to know I love him very much and want him to be able to talk to me about anything. Since that isn't the case, I pray that you can get to the root of his problems."

"Dad, I told you over and over, I don't have any problems, but yet you insist that I'm wrong." Joe said.

"Thanks for your input, Junior." They talked a few minutes longer about general things until Kristina said, "You can pick Joe up in forty-five minutes."

After Junior left, Kristina turned to Joe, "The first thing I need you to do is relax. I know this is a little unconformable for you, but you are going to be ok."

"I'm a little confused as to how to address you, auntie. I look at you and I see my auntie, but I know that I'm not here for a family visit." Joe responded.

"Joe, just relax. Would you like to sit here or go over to the sofa?"

"Here is ok."

"As for how you should address me, whatever makes you feel comfortable. I'm just here to hear you out. The first thing I like to let you know is whatever you tell me is between the two of us. I can't tell your dad or anyone else what goes on in our sessions without your permission. I do need to tell you that if I feel that you are a danger to yourself or anyone else I have to let the proper authorities know and your dad.

"You don't have to worry about that. I'm not in that kind of trouble. I know my dad is worry about me, but I'm just trying to work through a few things."

"Okay, we can start there if you like."

"So many things are going on right now. I really don't know where to start. When my Dad and I talked, he asked me a question I didn't know how to answer."

"What question was that?" Kristina asked.

"He asked me if I had a problem with Nika. I told him I didn't, but I'm not sure if that is the truth."

"Can you explain what you mean?"

"Well, I love my baby sister, and I'm happy to be a big brother. I always wished my parents had another child, so I wouldn't have felt so alone."

"So, if I'm hearing you correctly, you have mixed feelings about your baby sister because she isn't a child your Dad and Mom had together?"

"Yeah, I guess. I don't understand that feeling because I don't get along with my mom, and I like Alyssa. I guess I'm sad because I get less attention from Alyssa now that Nika is here."

"How does that make you feel?" Kristina was careful not to call Joe by his name so he wouldn't feel the need to say auntie.

"It makes me feel like I'm losing a mom again. I get mad at myself because Alyssa is still nice to me and try to keep our bond close, but all I seem able to focus on is, she is Nika's mom and not mine."

"Have you let Alyssa know how you were feeling?"

"No, I didn't want her to feel like I'm acting like a baby or jealous of Nika."

"Okay, is there anything else you would like to talk about?"

"Do you promise not to tell anyone?"

"I can't without your permission. Unless it is under the circumstances I explained earlier."

'Well, I made a big mistake that took care of itself, but it was terrifying,"

"What was that mistake?"

"Well, my dad asked me often about girls and we have talked about sex, drugs, and other problems that plague teenagers." Joe took a deep breath, "I got my best friend pregnant."

Kristina was taken aback. She had a feeling it was something big and life changing going on with Joe. "Ok, what do you mean by your mistake taking care of itself'

"Well, before we could decide what we were going to do, she lost the baby."

"I'm sorry for your lost. How are you and your friend handling this situation?

"This happened a few weeks ago. I only talked to her once and she has not come back to school yet. She was scared to tell her parents. I'm scared because I don't know what is going on with her."

"Your dad is going to be here in a few minutes. If you like to schedule another appointment to continue, I'm open."

"Auntie Kristy, I'm scare that Dad will be disappointed in me. I know we should have been more careful, but I really like Bria. Her name is Brianna but everyone calls her, Bria."

"Joe your dad loves you and will support you. Let him know what is going on with you. He will help you to figure things out."

"Auntie Kristy, I'm sorry, but I can't tell my dad. I don't want to lose him like I lost Mom."

"Joe, you didn't lose your mom. You know she loves you. She just needed to change her life so she could be happy."

"I will never forgive her. She walked out of my life and only wants to come back when it suits her." Joe said angrily.

The knock on the door let them know their time was up. Kristina told Junior to come in. Joe stood went over to Junior and gave him a hug.

"Dad, I'm not feeling good. Is it okay if I don't go to school today?" I'm caught up on all my work." Joe asked.

"Is everything okay, Joe?" Junior asked while looking at Kristina.

"Yes, Dad, everything is good. When can I schedule my next session with, Auntie Kristy?"

"That depends on your Auntie's schedule. Kristy what works for you?" Junior asked.

I can work something out where Joe could come in after school so he won't miss too many days. When do you want to come back?"

"Is it okay to come in on Tuesdays and Thursdays? I have things to do after school on the other days."

"Okay, I will put you down for Tuesday and Thursdays starting next week at three o'clock." Kristina said. She walked Junior and Joe to the door. When she went back to her office she was sadden because her nephew was going through so much and she couldn't talk to anyone about it.

Chapter Six

Junior sat in his office relaxing for a few minutes after the Monday morning meeting. It was hard for him to concentrate during the meeting. Diamond gave him a few impatient looks when it was his turn to present and he wasn't prepared. He felt so at a loss of how to help his family. He was so happy Saturday morning when Alyssa was finally released from the hospital. That afternoon his Dad and Bethany brought Nika home. Joe was a little distant, but he seemed glad that his step-mom and baby sister were home.

Junior hired a housekeeper, Mrs. Barnes, so Alyssa would have help while he was at work. Junior had to go home at lunchtime because now that Alyssa was home, Lance had to interview her about the accident. Just as a precaution, a detail team from the firm was assigned while Junior was at work. Junior wished Alyssa would open up to him. He knew there was more going on in her life than she was letting him know about. Even though he acted immature about the video, he apologized and asked her to be patient with him. He just wanted a life with no drama after dealing with Jalissa. Junior thought back to his conversation with Alyssa this morning.

"Alyssa, I don't want to pressure you since I know you're not up for it right now, but are you ready to talk about the accident?"

"Junior, I already told you, I don't remember much about what happened."

"Can you tell me where you were going or why you were on that side of town?"

"Can we talk about this later? Nika will be up soon, and I want to spend some time with her before I take a nap." Alyssa asked.

"Sure, Alyssa, but you're going to have to talk to Lance later. I'll be home around eleven 'o'clock."

On top of Alyssa and her secrets, Junior had to deal with Joe. He was glad that Joe was comfortable enough to talk to Kristina about his problems, but he wanted his son to talk to him. Junior knew Joe was still upset that Junior let him get his license, but refused to let him get a car or drive. Junior thought about that for a minute. *Was he being to hard on Joe?* Junior thought back to his senior year. He didn't have a car, but he also didn't deserve it because of his grades and behavior.

Joe was doing great in school. Keeping up with his grades and activities, while researching which university he wanted to attend. Maybe it was time Junior let go of his protectiveness. Since he wouldn't let Joe get a part-time job until the summer, Junior knew he and Alyssa would have to get the car. He thought about checking in with Jalissa, but changed his mind. The less contact he had with her was best for all involved. Jalissa had mellowed out, but he wasn't going to rock the boat. Junior was interrupted from his thoughts when there was a knock on his door. Junior stood when a pretty lady entered.

"Good morning." Junior said asking the lady to have a seat in front of his desk. He thought she looked familiar.

"Good morning. Sorry to drop by without an appointment, but I needed to speak to you right away." The mysterious lady said.

"Okay. What can I do to help you?"

"I need your help to contact my daughter."

"I can give you some referrals, but our firm usually don't take missing persons cases."

"My daughter isn't missing. I know exactly where she's living and so do you."

"I'm sorry, I don't understand. May I have your name please?"

"My name is Amanda Jones."

"Okay, Mrs. Jones, what do you mean when you say, I know exactly where your daughter is living?"

"No need for us to be so professional, Junior. After all we are family."

"I'm not following you." Junior said confused.

"Okay, let me break it down for you. You are my son-in-law. Alyssa is my daughter."

Junior was uncomfortable now. He knew Alyssa parents were deceased and she didn't have any other family members. "There must be some kind of misunderstanding; my wife doesn't have any living family members."

"That is where you are wrong, Junior. I'm very much alive and well. Alyssa and I have been estranged for years, until recently."

"Listen, Mrs. Jones, I have another appointment. I can't continue this conversation right now."

"Just give my daughter a message from me please. She can run, but she can't hide from the past." Amanda left Junior's office as quickly as she appeared. Junior sat baffled for a few minutes before he packed his things to head home to be with his wife for her interview with Lance.

Kristina sat in her office thinking about how she was going to approach her next appointment with Joe. She was still finding it difficult keep her personal life separated from her professional regarding his case. Seeing Joe as a patient instead of her nephew was difficult. The things they discussed on their first visit still disturbed her. Joe needed his dad now more than ever, but he refused to let Junior help. She didn't like keeping this from Junior, but she didn't have a choice.

Over the weekend when she was with Diamond and Dior she wanted so badly to let them in on what was going on. With Krystal coming home in a few days this will complicate things further. She will not want to respect that she couldn't talk about her sessions with Joe. Krystal would most likely blame Alyssa for Joe's problems. When her office line rang she answered it quickly.

"Good morning, Kristina's Kozy Korner."

"Auntie it's Joe."

"Hi, Joe. Why are you calling me on my work line?"

"Because I didn't want you to tell Dad that I'm not in school right now."

"Where are you, Joe?"

"I'm sitting across the street from Bria's house. I borrowed my friend's car."

"Why are you over there, Joe?"

"Because I need to know what is going on with Bria. I need to see and talk to her."

"Joe, I need you to take your friend's car back to him and I will meet you at the school."

"Auntie, I need to see and talk to her." Joe was almost in tears now.

"Joe we will find a way to work through this. Please take the car back. I will pick you up."

"Okay, please don't tell my dad, Auntie."

"Joe, we will talk when I pick you up."

"Okay, Auntie." Joe ended their call.

Kristina was at a loss. She couldn't call anyone to ask for advice and she couldn't call Junior even though that was what she wanted to do. Grabbing her purse and keys she headed to Joe's school.

Chapter Seven

When Junior arrived home he sat in the car for a few minutes thinking about his conversation with Amada Jones. Now that he had time to think, Amanda may have been telling the truth. Alyssa's features were similar, but what was more striking to Junior was how much Nika looked like the mystery lady. If this was true why would Alyssa tell him she didn't have any living family? He was under the impression she was alone in the world outside of her work family. She explained to him that is why she became involved with Kane Karter. His family adored her and that made her feel wanted.

Knowing he couldn't stay out there forever since Lance was due at any moment, Junior got out of the car and headed for the front door. As soon as he made it there, Lance pulled up behind him. Talking to Alyssa about his visitor before her interview wasn't going to happen to Junior's disappointment. The men greeted each other as Junior lead Lance into the family room. Alyssa was nowhere in sight so Junior figured she was upstairs with the baby. Mrs. Barnes offered to make them something for lunch, but Junior told her that wouldn't be necessary and she could have the rest of the day off.

Junior and Lance talked for about fifteen minutes, but when Alyssa didn't come down Junior went upstairs to see what was keeping her. When he arrived at their bedroom door, he heard her crying. Opening the door Junior was surprised to see her balled up in a fetal position rocking like she was in pain. Junior forgot all about Lance and being put out because Alyssa didn't come downstairs for her interview.

"Alyssa, baby what's wrong?" Junior asked. This was the first time since meeting her Junior saw her so vulnerable.

"Junior, I can't do this."

"You can't do what, baby?"

"I can't meet with Lance. My entire body is hurting. I need some sleep."

"Alyssa, Lance is only going to ask you a few questions. Let's get this over with, so we won't have to go down to the station."

"Didn't you hear what I said, Junior? I can't."

"Alyssa, please tell me what's going on with you."

"Nothing, Junior, tell Lance, I will come down to the station in the morning to make my statement."

"You should have told me this earlier, so I could have canceled the interview."

"Junior, I didn't know how exhausted I would be after giving Nika her bath."

Junior couldn't believe his ears. He hired a housekeeper, so Alyssa wouldn't have to do any of the heavy work. "Alyssa, you should have let Mrs. Barnes give the baby her bath?"

"I missed my baby and wanted to spend some time with her."

"I'll go talk to Lance." Junior left the room realizing he couldn't put off getting to the bottom of what was going on with his wife.

When Kristina arrived at the school, she didn't see Joe. He seemed to come out of nowhere to knock on her window. She could tell that he had been crying. She felt so bad for her nephew.

"Joe, are you okay?"

"No, Auntie. I don't know what to do. I sat at Brie's house for hours, but didn't see anyone coming or going."

"Joe, I think it is time for you to bring your dad into this, so he can help you."

"No, Auntie you promised. I don't want him to be mad at me. I think he is already mad at Alyssa."

"Why do you think your dad is mad at Alyssa, Joe?"

"Because of the way he talks to her. He isn't mean or anything he just not talking to her the way he normally talks to her."

"Even if that is the case, Joe, your dad loves you. You need to let him know what you are going through. He may even be able to reach out to Bria or her parents."

"No, that is the worst thing that could happen. I think the situation would get worst if the parents get involved."

"Joe, we can go back to my house to talk, but I do have to let your dad know that you are with me. He thinks you're at school. He has a right to know your whereabouts."

"Okay. But could you tell him that you will bring me home after we talk? I just need a little bit more time to see how to break the news to him."

"You're making the right decision, Joe. We are going to try something a little different today." Kristina said as she started up her car to head back to her office.

Chapter Eight

Junior decided to go back to his office after he told Lance that Alyssa would come in tomorrow morning to give her statement. He let Lance think that Alyssa wasn't feeling well physically, but Junior knew that it was emotional distress that was keeping Alyssa down. He had a feeling it had something to do with his visitor that was claiming to be her mother. His day didn't get any better when Kristina called and said that Joe was with her. She wouldn't go into any details, but she said Joe wasn't hurt or anything. Junior felt helpless that his wife or son wasn't being straight with him. A knock on his door broke up his sober mood.

"Come in."

"Junior, there is a, Mr. Morris waiting to see you. He doesn't have an appointment, but he said it was important." His assistant told him.

"Give me two minutes and send him in." Junior thought to himself. *"What the hell day was this, dump on Junior day."*

"Mr. Morgan, my name is Marcus Morris. I came to talk to you about my daughter, Brianna."

"It's nice to meet you, Mr. Morris, but if your daughter is missing, we don't handle missing person's cases."

"She's not missing, Mr. Morgan. She is safely tucked away to get away from her stalker."

"Again, this is an issue you should take to the police, Mr. Morris."

"I don't think you will be saying that when I tell you who her stalker is, Mr. Morgan."

"Please get to the point, Mr. Morris." Junior didn't want to play games with this man.

"Your son is the reason I had to send my daughter into hiding."

"What the hell are you talking about, Mr. Morris?"

What I'm talking about is your son getting my innocent sixteen year old daughter pregnant and hounding her until she had a miscarriage." Marcus Morgan said angrily.

"This isn't making any sense. My son wouldn't do something like that."

"Well, he did. I heard from my neighbors that he was staking out my house for hours today."

"I don't know anything about any of this, Mr. Morris. Rest assured I will be getting to the bottom of this. Please leave your contact information with my assistant. I promise to get back with you soon."

"Bria is trying her best to handle her lost. Please tell your son to leave her alone." Marcus left with a brief nod in Junior's direction.

Junior sat at his desk and prayed for a few minutes. He hoped with all his heart what Mr. Morris said wasn't true, but had to deal with the reality that may not be the case. He knew something had been bothering Joe for a long time, but every time he approached Joe, he would tell him nothing was wrong. Now Joe involved Kristina. Junior had to put a stop to this before it turned into a situation like the one Dillon was in a few years back. The family was almost torn apart because Dillon kept vital information private about Reggie. Well, he knew he couldn't put this off any longer so he packed his things and headed to Kristina's.

Kristina and Joe had only been at her house for about half an hour before Junior showed up. She didn't know if Joe could tell, but she could tell that Junior was trying his best to control his anger. She had to ask Junior a couple of times before he told her why he was there. When they talked over the phone earlier they agreed to let Kristina take

Joe home later when Reggie arrived home. As the three of them sat in her office, Kristina wanted to break the ice because she could see how tense Joe was getting in his dad's presence.

"Junior, Joe and I were just about to get started with a session. I thought we agreed I will bring Joe home later on."

"That would have been find, Kristy if I didn't received a visitor from an angry Dad saying that his daughter was been stalked."

All the blood seemed to drain out of Joe's face, but Kristina wanted to keep him calm.

"What does that have to do with your visit, Junior?"

Without answering Kristina's question Junior turned to face his son.

"Would you like to answer that question, Son?"

"Why would I know the answer to that question, Dad?" Joe asked.

"Does that name Marcus Morris ring a bell?"

Joe knew it was time to face the fact that he had to come clean with his Dad. "Yes, Dad, Mr. Morris is my friend Bria's, Dad."

"You care to tell me about this friend, Joe?"

Joe looked at Kristina before he answered. "Well, Dad, Bria is a girl I like at school."

"Have you been stalking her?"

"No, I haven't, Dad."

"That isn't what her dad is saying."

"I haven't seen her for a few weeks. I was worried about her that's all, Dad."

"Tell me the whole story right now, Joe."

"I like her, she stopped coming to school and I've been worried."

Junior stood and started pacing. "Cut the crap, Joe. Mr. Morris said that you got his sixteen year old daughter pregnant and hounded her so much she lost her baby."

Joe put his hands over his face and started crying. Kristina wanted to put an end to this, but she knew the entire story had to come out.

"I'm sorry, Dad. We only had sex one time and I thought I had the condom on right, but I guess I didn't."

"Joe, we have talked about sex many times and I asked you to tell me when you became active. Why didn't you?"

"I was scared, Dad. You are the only parent, I have left. Mom doesn't care, Nana is gone and my grandparents don't understand me."

"Stop with the self-pity, Joe. You made a grown decision when you decided to have sex with that girl, so you're going to have to take responsibility."

"Junior, maybe it's a good idea to take Joe home to finish this discussion." Kristina suggested.

"Auntie, can we stay here to talk?"

"No, Joe, we're going home. Kristy, I appreciate all your help."

"Before you guys leave, Joe this situation may become a legal issue. Is it okay for me to talk to your, Auntie Di about what is going on?"

"Kristie, why do you think this will become a legal issue?" Junior asked.

"I'm not comfortable with the way Bria's, dad stopped by your office unannounced. He may have something else on his mind and was just trying to feel you out."

"It's okay to talk to her, Auntie. I'm sure soon the whole family will know." Joe said sadly.

"Thanks for giving me permission, Joe. I just want to be prepared if the worst happens." Kristina walked Junior and Joe to Junior's car, and then went back to her office to gather her thoughts before she talked to Diamond.

Chapter Nine

Diamond sat at her desk early Wednesday morning wondering why Kristina wanted to see her. Kristina wouldn't give her any details over the phone. Diamond knew it had to be important because Kristina cancel two of her morning sessions. Diamond prayed it wasn't Reggie. Dillon told her Reggie was back to his old self, but she didn't know what would trigger another manic episode. Hearing the knock on her door brought her back to the present.

"Good morning, Di. Thanks for seeing me on such short notice." Kristina said.

"Not a problem, sis. Is everything alright at home?"

"Come on, Di. Is the family ever going to forget about Reg's situation?"

"Kristy, we care about you. You can't expect us to feel one hundred percent confident after what happen."

"Reg is great. Joe on the other hand is having a few issues."

"Junior mentioned a while back he was worried about Joe, but since he hadn't said anything else. I thought things had gotten better."

"Well, they haven't, Di." I need you not to get upset about what I'm about to tell you."

"Spit it out, Kristy."

"Joe has been in counseling with me and..."

"Wait, hold up, Kristy. I know you're not telling me you took Joe on as a patient?"

"Yes, I have, Di." Kristina responded.

"I'm going to kill, Junior. Why the hell would he ask you to do something like that, Kristy? If Joe needed counseling he should have asked you for a referral." Di stood from her desk and started pacing around the room.

"I thought about that, Di. I didn't make this decision lightly, but Joe wouldn't agree to go to another counselor."

"That's too damn bad. Have you forgotten what happen when Dillon helped Reggie?"

"No, Di, I haven't forgotten."

"On top of that you're pregnant. I know Reggie wasn't onboard with you taking Joe's case."

"No, he wasn't, but what was I supposed to do? Junior was so sad and with all that he's going through with Alyssa, he didn't need any added stress."

"What's going on with Joe, Kristy?" Diamond asked as she sat back down.

"Well, the short of the situation is, he got his girlfriend pregnant. Her Dad said Joe stalked her until she lost the baby. Joe is worried sick about Bria."

"Unbelievable, I know Junior talked to that boy about safe sex. How the hell did he let that happen?"

"Di, there's more. Joe is confused about his home situation too. He doesn't know why he feels like Alyssa abandon him when she had Nika."

"Kristy, call Junior right now and tell him you are going to refer Joe's case."

"I can't do that, Di. Joe needs me right now. I promise not to overdo it, but I can't give up on him now, he is a mess."

"What made you tell me about this, Kristy?"

"Well, with the visit from Mr. Morris, I thought this may become a legal matter. At first, Joe wouldn't let me tell anyone about our sessions."

"That's the point, Kristy. How did it make you feel when you had to keep this from Junior?"

"It felt like I was betraying our brother." Kristina said with tears in her eyes.

"Exactly, what if something more disturbing comes up in a session?"

"I already explained to, Joe if I felt he was a danger to himself or anyone else or broke the law I would have to alert professionals and tell his dad."

"Kristy, again, I'm going to advise you to cut your losses. You were right about trouble from Bria's, dad. Money may not be an issue since she is going to the same private school as Joe, but helpless parents can make this situation difficult for Junior and Joe."

"Di, I have to get back home. Thanks for seeing me. I will think about everything we discussed. I know I'm going to be in trouble with Mom and Dad when Junior tells them about this situation."

"Don't worry about that, Kristy. Text me when you get home. Make sure you get some rest." Diamond walked Kristina to her car. When she returned to her desk she prepared herself for family drama.

Dior had forgotten how bad rush hour traffic could be as she made her way to pick Krystal up from the airport. She hoped Krystal would be too tired to want the run down on the family. Alyssa's situation didn't sit well with the rest of the family, but for Krystal she was going to make a federal case out of it and of course blame it all on Alyssa.

Dior was worried about Junior. He mentioned a few problems he was having with Joe, so with Alyssa's problems on top of that he had to be exhausted. Charlie advised Dior to let Junior come to her if he needed help. That was hard for Dior. She remembered how supportive Junior was to her when she went through the fire at her daycare. He was having big problems with Jalissa, but he still found the time to be there for her. Arriving at the airport, she was there about half hour before Krystal plane landed and almost another hour before they were headed back to their parents' house.

"Okay, Dior, give me the scoop on what I've missed." Krystal said.

"Mom and Dad are doing great. He is still driving her crazy since he doesn't have anything to keep him busy since Nika went back home."

"Well, if you ask me, Nika should stay with Mom and Dad for a little while. Maybe that would give Junior enough alone time with that woman to see it's time to call it quits."

"Krystal Ann Morgan, don't you dare say anything like that to our brother. He is having a hard enough time without you being so negative towards his wife."

"I'm not going to say it like that, Dior, but someone needs to tell him to be careful."

"Not you, baby girl. You will get too much enjoyment out of his misery."

"Let's change the subject. How is, Kristy doing? I hope she is taking it easy. Just because she is not on any restrictions with this baby doesn't mean she can forget about taking care of herself."

"Kristy is good. She has already cut back on her practice."

"What about the perfect couple."

"Stop hating, Krystal. Di and Dillon are doing well too."

"I'm not hating, Dior. It's still rubs me the wrong way that Dillon won't let up on me. Whenever he sees me, he has this funny look on his face."

"That's your guilty conscious talking. What do you expect when you almost got his wife killed?"

"I expect for him to forgive me and notice how much I'm trying to do better with my life. He acts like he doesn't even want me to volunteer at the center."

"He will come around, baby girl. Now tell me how you been doing." Dior and Krystal talked the rest of the way to their parent's house about Krystal's work and how nauseating it was to see Kendra and Kane so happy.

Chapter Ten

It had been almost a week since Alyssa been home from the hospital and she still hadn't talked to Junior about the accident. When he took her in to see Lance at the station the other day she asked him to wait for her in the lobby. He still hadn't been able to talk to her about the woman who said she was her mom. Junior needed answers so he told Diamond he was taking the morning off. She was under the impression it was about Joe and Junior wasn't in the mood to clarify. Sitting on the bed in their bedroom, Junior waited for Alyssa to come into the room after taking her shower. He had already asked Mrs. Barnes to keep an eye on Nika.

"Alyssa, we have to talk?"

"Junior, I have to go take care of the baby."

"No, you don't. I asked Mrs. Barnes to keep an eye on her."

"Now isn't a good time to talk, Junior."

"You have been saying that since you got home from the hospital, Alyssa, so that is not going to wash any longer."

"Junior, let's talk later."

Junior ignored Alyssa's last comment and proceeded with the conversation, "Alyssa, I had a visit from Amanda Jones."

Alyssa dropped the brush she was using to brush her hair, "Excuse me, Junior." Alyssa ran into the bathroom.

Junior was dumbfounded. He didn't know what to do. Alyssa's face looked as though she saw a ghost. Junior knew for sure that what Amanda said was true. She was Alyssa's mom. He waited fifteen minutes for Alyssa to come out of the bathroom. When she didn't, Junior went to knock on the door.

"Alyssa, please come out and talk to me."

"Junior, I can't do this right now."

Junior could tell that Alyssa was crying. "I'm not going anywhere until we talk this out, Alyssa." Junior said. A few minutes later Alyssa walked pass Junior and sat on the bed.

"Junior, I don't know what that lady told you, but she is not my mother. She is just the person I was unlucky enough to be born to."

"Alyssa, why did you tell me your mom was dead?"

"She is dead to me, Junior."

"What's going on Alyssa? I think you owe me an explanation."

"Well, as you know, the woman that gave birth to me is not dead. Up until three months ago I hadn't seen here since I was fourteen years old."

"What, happened, baby. You know I will support you. I want to hear the whole story."

"Mandy, is my biological mom. She never told me anything about my bio dad. I'm sure that is because she doesn't know who my dad is because she was a hooker."

"Why, didn't you tell me about her, Alyssa?"

"I wanted to forget she existed. She is a horrible person. When I was fourteen, I was adopted by the Addams family. I considered them my parents. They died when I was in college. I was devastated."

"Why didn't you tell me you were adopted?"

"I just wanted to forget about my early childhood. My adopted parents loved me unconditionally and left me well off when they died."

"You said that three months ago you were reunited with your biological mom. Why didn't you let me know what you were going through?"

"I'm embarrassed. You see what a mess that woman is, Junior."

"We can't be talking about the same woman. The woman that came to see me was nicely dressed and spoke like she was educated." Junior said.

"That's because she has been draining money from me. Money I know she didn't need. Underneath the nice clothes and fake pretense of being someone important, she is the same woman that sold me to her pimp when I was fourteen."

Junior couldn't believe his ears, "Your, Mom sold you to her pimp?"

"Yes, Junior, if I didn't run away, I would have ended up in the same boat she was in."

"How did she find you after all these years?" Junior asked.

"When the video tape was released of Kane and me, she contacted me about a week later."

"How did she make you give her money?"

"She threatened to go public about our relationship and to let the public know I was in the same profession. I wasn't going to let her do that to you, Joe, and our daughter." Alyssa was sobbing now. She couldn't tell Junior the entire story right now.

"I need you to be totally honest with me, Alyssa. Did she have anything to do with the accident or why you and Nika was on that side of town?"

Sobbing even more, when Alyssa finally calmed down she said, "Junior, I couldn't take her any longer."

"What were you planning on doing, Alyssa?"

"I was trying to run away from her."

"I don't care about that, Alyssa. Do you think I wouldn't have come to look for both of you?"

"I wasn't thinking, Junior. I just needed to get away."

"How, do you expect for me to trust or help you, if you don't tell me what's going on, Alyssa?"

"Junior, I'm feeling sick. I need to rest for a little while." Alyssa moved to the head of the bed. In a fetal position she sobbed quietly.

"I'll talk to you later, Alyssa." Junior left the bedroom and headed out of the house.

After leaving the house Junior called his dad to see if he could meet him. He didn't want to go to his house. He knew his dad was going to tell Bethany what they talked about, but he just wanted private time with his dad. He also didn't want to deal with Krystal right now.

He talked to her a few time since she returned home and all she talked about, was when was he going to end his marriage to Alyssa. His dad agreed to meet him at a small café around the corner from the firm. Once they arrived Nick got straight to the point.

"What happened, Son? Is Joe okay?" Nick and Bethany was upset when they found out Kristina was counseling Joe.

"Joe is fine, Dad. It's Alyssa, she has a mom, she didn't tell me about."

"I thought her parents were deceased?" Nick said.

"Yeah, I did too, come to find out the Addams were her adopted parents. Her biologically mother is alive and well. As matter a fact, Nika looks a lot like her."

"Why didn't Alyssa tell you about this before you guys got married?"

"She said she wanted to forget about that part of her life. She said her mom is a hooker that sold Alyssa to her pimp when she was fourteen."

"Get the hell out of here. You mean to tell me, she thought it was okay to keep this to herself?"

"Yes, she did, Dad."

"What else is she hiding?"

"Apparently, Amanda has been blackmailing her. On the day of the accident she was planning on leaving me and taking Nika with her."

"What do you plan to do about this, Junior? She had to have known that you would have gone looking for your daughter."

""Dad, I would have looked for both of them. I love my wife."

"Junior, you can't get yourself in the same position you were in with Jalissa. That woman almost destroyed you." Nick said.

"Dad, Alyssa isn't Jalissa. She is more grounded and since I met her this is the first time I seen her lose control."

"Be that as it may, you need to make sure she doesn't take your daughter away."

"I will think of something. I'm also in the process of convincing Joe to see another therapist. I should have done that from the start, but I was just so worried about him."

"It seems to me that your wife and son needs a little fear put into them. Why would she think it is okay to take my grandchild away? As for Joe, if he wants to make grown up decisions he needs to man up. You shouldn't have to convince him to see another therapist."

"Dad, he's been through a lot with me and Jalissa going at each other all the time."

"I understand that, Son, but that doesn't give him the right to dictate what he is going to do. Put your foot down and tell Kristy to make a referral or find one on your own. I'm sure your assistant can take care of that for you."

"Okay, Dad, I know what I need to do. Thanks for meeting with me. I'll keep you posted." Junior paid the check and they went their separate ways.

Chapter Eleven

Junior sat in his office talking to Alyssa after his Monday morning meeting. Things had gotten a little better for them. Alyssa apologized to him when he returned from his visit with his dad a few days ago. Junior didn't know how to take her apology, because he knew she still wasn't upfront with him about everything. He made it clear to her that if she wanted out, she wasn't taking his daughter. That pissed her off a little, but she understood, because she wouldn't want Junior to take Nika away from her either. Junior's desk phone ranged. He told his assistant to send the visitor in. Alyssa was upset to see Amanda.

"What the hell are you doing here, lady?"

"I told you to watch how you speak to me, girl. How are you doing son-in-law?" Amanda asked.

"Why are you here, Mrs. Jones?"

"We don't have to be so formal. Call me Amanda or Mandy."

"We don't have anything to say to you, so please leave." Alyssa said.

"I want to see my granddaughter."

"It would be a cold day in hell before I let that happen." Alyssa responded.

"Lyssa, you need to let the past be in the past. I told you things are different with me now."

Alyssa ignored Amanda and spoke directly to Junior, "You need to have that lady thrown out or I'm leaving."

Junior had never seen this side to Alyssa. She was cold and hateful and all he could think about was how bad the last few years of his marriage to Jalissa had been. "Ladies, we need to calm down and come to an understanding. Mrs. Jones, I agree with Alyssa, now isn't the right time to see the baby. You and Alyssa need to work out your differences before exposing Nika to a hostile environment."

"Lyssa, I'm not playing with you. I will see my granddaughter again." Amanda persisted.

"What do you mean again?" Junior asked.

"Didn't Lyssa tell you, I met my granddaughter on the day of the accident? Lyssa it isn't good to keep secrets from your husband."

"No, she didn't." Junior replied angrily.

Alyssa stood went across the room and slapped Amanda so hard Junior felt it. "Don't ever come near me or my family again. Now get the hell out of here or I'll throw you out."

"You're going to regret that, you ungrateful, Bitch." Amanda left the room after giving Alyssa a dirty look.

"Alyssa, that wasn't called for, why did you hit your mom?"

"I told her to leave us the hell alone. Since she doesn't understand words I thought I would speak her language."

"I have to get back to work. Let's finish this up at home later." Junior didn't give Alyssa a chance to answer. He escorted her by the arm to the front door of the building, kissed her lightly on the forehead, and then went back into his office.

Later that afternoon Kristina was having her last session with Joe. She was happy she was able to convince him to see one of her referrals. She assured him that he could still talk to her whenever he needed to, but to avoid family conflict she needed to step away. She also let him know that she have to let his dad know what they talk about if she felt he needed to know. Diamond already reached out to Bria's parents who informed her that their daughter would not be going back to that school and they wanted Joe to discontinue any contact with her. That is where Kristina wanted to start their session off with, first she wanted Joe to relax.

"Okay, we're going to start off with a breathing technique. I want you to take a deep breath and let it out. We are going to do that three times." After they were done with breathing, Kristina asked Joe how he was feeling.

"I feel relaxed right now, but I've been anxious since my dad found out what happened with Bria. I'm just waiting on him to send me packing to my mom or her parents."

"Why do you feel your dad want to send you away?"

"I feel that because, he's been concerned about me, but in a different way."

"Can you explain that a little better to me?"

"Well, he doesn't give me his full attention when we're talking. I get the feeling that he just wants me to hurry up and say what I have to say so he could move on to something else."

"Have he ever told you he didn't have time to listen to you?'

"No, but he is going through something heavy with, Alyssa."

"Is that why you feel he doesn't have time for you?"

"Partly, but for the most part I feel he is disappointed in me."

"Are you feeling guilty about how your actions may have affected your family?"

"Yes. To be cut off from Bria was hard enough, but I'm worried about how the rest of the family will treat me. I feel like a failure." Joe said as the tears rolled down his face.

"Let's take a minute to relax. I need you to close your eyes. I want you to take a few breaths in and out. Now I want you to tell me, where do you see yourself ten years from now?" Kristina asked.

"Hard to say, I hope to have a good job." Joe responded.

"What about success. Do you see yourself as being successful?"

"Yes. I want to go into law, but not criminal like auntie and granddad. I want to help keep families together."

"Why does that mean so much to you?"

"I want to make it my life's work to save as many kids as possible from the kind of life I had."

"What do you mean by that?"

"Well, I wished Nana was in my life when I was little. I miss her so much. We didn't have that much time together. I don't want any kid to have to live is a house like I grew up with my parents. I saw before my eyes my mom went from supportive and loving to mean and hateful."

"What kind of lifestyle do you see yourself living?"

"Well, since I have my choice of six universities giving me a full ride, I want to live off my trust fund so it would allow me to donate time to disadvantage kids."

"That is great. I want you to relax again and slowly open your eyes." Kristina watched Joe closely. "How are you feeling now?"

"I feel refreshed. I can't believe how you got me to say so much. I've been keeping so much bottled in I was afraid I was going to explode."

"Joe, the next therapist may do something similar to this with you. Just remember to always be honest and express what you are feeling. Your sessions should be a place where you don't feel like you have to hold anything back."

"Auntie Kristy, thank you so much. I know I put you in a bad position, but you stood by me and I appreciate that so much."

"Joe the entire family is here for you. Your dad is awesome so please be honest with him."

"I will try harder. I just want him to be happy because he deserves it after losing Nana and my mom being so mean to him."

"Joe, what happened between your mom and dad is up to them to work out. You may want to cut your mom some slack. Over the last few years she has fought hard to get her life back in order."

"I know, but she abandoned me to do that. I feel she could have found a better way to change her life."

"Your dad will be here in a few minutes. Let's wrap this up for now. Good luck with your new therapist, and I will always be here for you." Kristina and Joe made small talked until Junior picked him up.

Chapter Twelve

Junior was at his breaking point with Alyssa and her mom. There had to be a lot more going on for her to despise her mom. He tried to talk to her all week about what was going on, but she continued to shut him out. Now it was Friday morning, he refused to go into another weekend with unanswered questions. He took the day off from work and decided to confront Alyssa again once she put Nika down for her nap.

"Alyssa, I need to know what happened on the day of the accident."

"Junior, I know we need to talk about this, but we're going to have to wait until we won't be interrupted."

"That can easily be arranged. Mrs. Barnes will be back in about thirty minutes. She can keep an eye Nika so we can go someplace private to talk." Junior said.

"Amanda is a hot mess. I don't want to have anything to do with that woman."

"That's understandable, Alyssa, but there was no reason for you to get physical. That side of you made me very uncomfortable."

"Have she tried to contact you, Junior?"

"No, I haven't heard a word from her since our last meeting."

"That is what concerns me, for her to think she has a right to see our daughter or be a part of our lives is ridiculous."

"Alyssa, maybe she is sick or something and wants to make amends."

"I don't care what the reason is for her return. If she died today I wouldn't miss her?"

"Do you hear how horrible you sound?"

"I'm waiting on a report to see why she is here. I should have done that as soon as she had the nerve to contact me."

"You're having your mom investigated." Junior asked shock.

"You damn right I am. I hope to find something I can use to lock her ass up and throw away the key."

"I can't talk to you when you get this way. Please come to the office as soon as Mrs. Barnes gets back." Junior left the house before he said something to his wife he couldn't take back.

Diamond sat in her office working on a new case. She knew this case was going to take up a lot of her time. She thought about Kristina and was so happy she decided to refer Joe's case to a therapist. The rift this could have caused the family was frightening. She knew Junior wasn't happy with Kristina's decision, but he accepted that she had to do what was right for her and the family. The knock on the door brought Diamond out of her thoughts. Telling her assistant to come in without looking up from her paperwork, she wondered why she was hesitating.

"Di, there is a woman out here that won't take no for an answer when I told her you couldn't see her without an appointment."

"Why is she here?"

"She wouldn't say, just said that it was about a personal family matter.

"Now, what the hell is going on. What is her name?"

"Mrs. Jones."

"Okay, give me two minutes and send her in." Diamond hoped this didn't have anything to do with Joe's ex-girlfriend. She had a feeling they hadn't heard the last of that family. When a beautiful older woman walked in Diamond paused. She looked familiar, but Diamond couldn't place where they would have met.

"Hi, Mrs. Washington, my name is Amanda Jones."

"Mrs. Jones, I'm very busy. Why are you here?" Diamond didn't have time to waste.

"I'm here about my granddaughter."

"What about your granddaughter. We don't handle missing persons' cases here."

"My granddaughter isn't missing, her parents is giving me a hard time about seeing her."

"Again, we can't help you here. If you check with my assistant she can give you a list of attorneys that would be able to assist you."

"I came to you because I don't think you would want your family dragged through the mud." Amanda said.

"Look, I don't know what your game plan is, but you need to leave. I don't have time for this nonsense."

"Oh well, I thought you would have more sense than your brother. I guess I was wrong."

"What does this have to do with my brother?"

"I've attempted to get him to see reason more than once, but he wants to back up my hateful daughter."

Wow, now Diamond knew why this lady looked so familiar. She had to be Alyssa's (supposed to be dead mom). Nika features strongly resembled her grandmother's. Before Diamond could address Amanda, Junior knocked on her door and slowly entered. He had his head down looking over a report Diamond hoped was the one she asked for a few days ago.

"Di, I'm finally done…" That was all he got out before walking into the office and facing Amanda. "What the hell are you doing here, Amanda?" Junior asked.

"Junior, what is going on here?" Diamond didn't like drama in her place of work.

"Di, I'm sorry she disturbed you. Amanda, I need you to follow me to my office please." Junior insisted.

"She isn't going anywhere until one of you let me know what the hell is going on here." Diamond shouted.

"Di, I don't know the entire story. I expect Alyssa here shortly to bring me up to date."

"Good luck with that one. She is too stuck-up to open up to anyone." Amanda said.

"I won't have you disrespecting my wife like that, Amanda."

"Disrespect, what about when she physically attacked me in your office. You didn't do a damn thing to stop her."

"Junior, when Alyssa gets here, we're going to meet in the conference room. You should have told me what was going on with you guys."

"Di calm down. I have everything under control." Junior said, while shooting Amanda a dirty look.

"You don't control anything. Lyssa won't let anyone control her."

"Junior, I need you to take Mrs. Jones to the conference room. I will let your assistant know to send Alyssa there when she arrives. I will be with you guys in a few minutes." Diamond didn't have time for this shit, but knew she had to get things under control before they have a mess on their hands. After Junior and Amanda left her office Diamond jotting down a few notes for the case she was working on, and prepared herself for an emotional battle between Junior, Alyssa, and Amanda.

Chapter Thirteen

Junior realized there was a lot he didn't understand and know about his wife. He couldn't believe it when he found out at their meeting that Alyssa had planned to take his daughter out of the country. She tried to explain that she wanted to keep her safe from Amanda, but he didn't care about that explanation. As he sat waiting on his dad, he thought back to the meeting earlier that day.

"Junior, I'm disappointed that you didn't let me know what was going on in the office. I don't want to interfere in your private life, but when it affects our firm, that is not acceptable." Diamond said.

"Di, don't blame Junior. This is her fault." Alyssa said pointing towards Amanda.

"You better stop disrespecting me, you spoil ass brat." Amanda responded.

"Alyssa, whatever problems you two have, you better keep it far away from here." Diamond said.

"I'm sorry, Di. As you can see this person thinks she can do whatever she wants. Junior if she comes back around here I suggest you call the police."

"If I go to jail, you best believe I'll be taking your sorry ass with me." Amanda threatened.

"Wait a minute. What are you talking about Amanda?" Junior asked.

"You want to tell him or shall I, daughter dearest."

"Junior, she is making a big deal about something that wasn't going to happen. She thinks I was going to take Nika and leave the country."

"Why, would she think that, Alyssa?"

"I can answer for myself. I think that because that is what she told me. I saw the passports in her car." Amanda explained.

"I just told her that so she could leave me alone. I wasn't going to take our daughter out of the country without your permission." Alyssa tried to defend herself.

"Liar, yes you were." Amanda persisted.

"We don't have time for this back and forth. Alyssa, you know that you would have been charged with kidnapping if you took Nika away without Junior's permission." Diamond said.

"I know the law, Di."

"Alyssa, did your mom play a role in the accident that could have killed our daughter?" Junior asked.

"Yes, that stupid ass woman jumped in the car with me and grabbed the wheel while I was driving. I didn't want to say anything because I wanted to leave her where she belongs, in the past."

"This is too much. Di, I'm sorry this took place in the office. Amanda, do not come here again. If you do I'm going to have you arrested. Alyssa, I'll talk to you later." Junior left the conference room.

Now that his Dad arrived, Junior knew it was time for him to pay the piper. "Look, Dad, I know Di told you what happened at the office. I have taken care of the situation."

"If you call taking care of the situation as assuring me that your personal life won't be brought into the office again, we have nothing to talk about." Nick said.

"I'm not defending Alyssa's actions, but Amanda put her in a terrible situation."

"Yes, one where she could have taken my granddaughter out of the country to God knows where."

"That aspect bothered me too, Dad. I still don't think she would have gone through with it. She was just reacting to a bad situation."

"Take the blinders off, Son. Of course she would have gone through with it. I'm starting to think that, Krystal was right about Alyssa's character."

"Dad, Krystal in the last person in the world that should judge anyone. The family has given her so many chances. Di almost lost her life because of the poor choices she made."

"This isn't about your sister, Junior, this is about your wife keeping secrets from you and the family."

"We are going to handle this, Dad. There is no need for the family to get involved or worry about something bad happening."

"I have to get back home. Thanks for letting the baby stay with us for a while. The house is quiet when she isn't there. Also, Beth is starting to worry about the baby's safety."

"Tell, Mama Beth, all is well. Thanks again for everything, Dad." Junior walked with his dad as they headed to the office to see how things were going.

"We got to do something quick. My marriage is falling apart." Alyssa said.

"It shouldn't be much longer. We can't give up on the operation now. We have to move on to Phase Two."

"Skip Phase Two. I can't afford to take baby steps any longer. My daughter and possible other family members are in danger."

"The worst thing you can do right now is panic."

"That is easy for you to say when you don't have anything to lose."

"We both know that is not true. I just don't have as much as you, but I don't want to lose what I've gained over the last year."

"Well, the target is set up perfectly right now, so we need to move while we have momentum on our side."

"If this goes down like we plan this will be one of the biggest bust in the last ten years."

"I don't care about that. I am out no matter how this case turns out."

"Okay, you made your point."

"Affirmative, until then take care." Alyssa ended the meeting and headed home to her family.

Chapter Fourteen

Junior had a lot on his mind. He had just finished up the Monday morning meeting and was trying to put the rest of his day in order. He had to leave work early today so he could take Joe to his first counseling appointment with the new therapist. Joe seemed to have mellowed since his few sessions with Kristina. He didn't want to start up with the new therapist, but knew he didn't have a choice.

Junior appreciated the quiet weekend he shared with his family. The baby was growing like a spud and Alyssa seemed more at peace. He decided to leave the subjects of the accident and her bio mom alone for the time being. He wished he had more family support. He felt like only Kristina understood him. He and Diamond used to be so close, but he felt the situation with Alyssa, and his asking Kristina to counsel Joe created a rift in their relationship.

To set his dad and step-mom mind at ease, Junior agreed to an in-depth investigation of Alyssa. His dad had somewhat did that when he knew Junior was interested in Alyssa, but with the recent events Nick didn't want to take any chances. Junior had mixed feelings about carrying on with the investigation, but in the end he wanted to know more about his wife. Diamond had misgivings saying that Alyssa left her life back in New York too easily. Diamond liked and respected Alyssa more than anyone in his family, so for her to have misgivings was saying a lot.

Looking at his watch, Junior had around fifteen minutes to kill before he met with the investigator that was going to handle Alyssa's case. He was nervous about Joe's appointment. He felt the need to bring Jalissa up to date, but Joe didn't want him to, saying his mom didn't care. Instead of calling Jalissa, Junior decided to call Kristina.

"Hi, big brother, how is your day going so far."

"Well, I'm a little anxious about Joe's appointment today. He has gone from obsessing over Bria to acting like it doesn't matter that he can't communicate with her."

"He's at an undefinable stage in his life. He's not a kid any longer, but he not an adult, but he has to deal with adult issues because of the choices he has made." Kristina explained.

"At least we had a good weekend. Both he and Alyssa seemed more at ease and really liked our family time together."

"Mom and Dad wondered why you guys weren't at church yesterday. Dad told me about his and Krystal's misgivings about Alyssa and his talk with you."

"I appreciate the family's concern, but Dad needs to chill and Krystal has no right to judge anyone."

"Junior, you shouldn't get mad at the family for showing concern. We are worried about the safety of all you guys. You know I like Alyssa, I just hope something from her past isn't going to bring trouble to the family."

"I understand all of that, Kristy, but let's change the subject. How is your pregnancy going?"

"I feel great. I'm not tired all the time like I was with Miracle and the doctor expects me to have a safe and normal delivery. Reg is still being over-protective."

"That is great, Kristy. I'm just a little put out with myself for adding the burden of Joe's treatment on you. I thought Di was going to hang me for that move."

"I wanted to help. If I wasn't pregnant I would have fought the family harder. Even though everything is going good, I don't want to take any chances."

"Okay, sis, I've taken up too much of your time. Thanks for the talk and I'll let you know how Joe's first appointment went later this evening." Junior ended his call with Kristina and decided to get back to work.

Dior sat in her office at the daycare waiting on Krystal to arrive. She loved her baby sister, but she hoped she didn't want to have an Alyssa bashing party. Dior had her concerns about Alyssa too, but since Junior was so happy and settled she prayed that Alyssa wouldn't do anything to hurt her brother. Coming out of her thoughts when she felt someone watching her, Dior stood from her desk and gave her baby sister a hug.

"I stood there forever waiting for you to notice I had arrived." Krystal said.

"Good afternoon to you too, baby sister."

"What were you thinking about?"

"Our family, hoping there isn't another crisis on the horizon."

"I know you have to be talking about, Alyssa. That chic is the worst thing that has happened to our family in years."

"Stop overreacting, Krystal. You need to let go of your grudge against Alyssa."

"She is hiding something, dad agrees with me."

"Let's pray she's not..." Dior stopped mid statement when Alyssa walked into the office with Annika.

"Good afternoon, ladies. Sorry to interrupt. Can Nika stay here for a few hours, Dior? Junior will pick her up after he gets off work." Alyssa asked.

"Sure she can. Is everything ok?" Dior responded.

"Yes, something important came up. We gave the housekeeper the day off, and I didn't want to bother your parents on short notice.

"You could have at least called before coming over." Krystal said.

"Cut it out, Krystal. Nika is welcome here anytime."

"When are you going to grow the hell up, Krystal?" Alyssa asked.

"Let's see." Krystal thought for a minute. "I guess that will be when you get the hell out of my brother's life."

"Don't pretend you care about, Junior. You treat him like dirt on the bottom of your high priced shoes."

"Ladies, that's enough, Alyssa you can take Nika to the infant care room to sign her in." Dior interceded. When Alyssa left the room Dior continued, "Why do you have to be so mean to her, Krystal?"

"I don't like her, and I'm not going to pretend that I do. We probably would have been better off if Junior stayed with ghetto ass Jalissa."

"That's wasn't our decision it was Junior's. When Alyssa comes back you need to apologize to her. She has been through a lot and I'm sure she hasn't fully recovered from the accident."

"Sorry, Sis, that's not going to happen. I know there is more going on, and she is putting this family in danger." Krystal said as Alyssa walked back into Dior's office, said goodbye to Dior, and rolled her eyes at Krystal.

Chapter Fifteen

Alyssa sat at the kitchen table looking at the door that her husband just departed. Things were a little better between them, but she didn't have faith that her marriage was going to survive. She wished she had someone to talk to. The only Morgan sister she felt she could be open with was Kristina. Even though she was closer to Diamond, she had to be careful with every single word that came out of her mouth when she was around her. Diamond's legal mind never seemed to shut down.

The meeting she had a few days ago made her faced the reality that she was not going to be able to keep up with her assignment and save her marriage. She knew a choice had to be made, so she decided to ditch her life's work to be with the man she loved and their family. She hadn't heard anything from Amanda and for that she was grateful. She knew that lady was up to no good.

Knowing it was time to come clean about everything she asked Diamond to stop by this morning. Their conversation wasn't going to be easy, so she asked Nick and Bethany to take Annika for a few days so she and Diamond could deal with the situation she found herself knee deep in. Thinking back to the time when she made the biggest mistake in her life was short lived when she heard the doorbell ring and knew Diamond had arrived. She had to answer it because she given Mrs. Barnes the day off since the baby wasn't there. Leading Diamond into the family room, Alyssa was uncomfortable for the first time with her sister-in-law.

"Alyssa, you want to tell me why you wanted to meet with me this morning?" Diamond asked.

"Di, I don't want to put you in a bad position, but I need to talk to you as my attorney, not my sister-in-law."

"I've been thinking about that Alyssa. I find myself in the same position Kristy was in when she was counseling Joe." Diamond paused to get her thoughts together. "I don't want to strain my relationship with my brother by keeping something a secret that he should know about. When you talked to the police without me, I felt relieved because my gut is telling me that Junior is in for heartbreak."

"Di, I hope you won't back out on me now. I don't want to come between you and the family, but I need your help badly." Alyssa said.

"Whatever you holding back from Junior will it put any of my family in harm's way?"

"Possibly, it's almost over. I just need to run the entire case by you so I can move on with my life with Junior and the kids."

"Before you tell me anything, the only promise I can make to you is if any of my family members are in danger I will do whatever needs to be done to protect them."

"So your answer is no. Our talk will not be attorney-to-client?"

"I'm sorry, Alyssa. I won't do anything to betray my family. Over the years we have been through too many cover-up situations that could have torn the family apart."

"Well, I'm sorry I wasted your time, Di. I need a little more time to see things through."

As Diamond was getting ready to leave she said, "Alyssa, you are important to this family. Please be honest with Junior sooner rather than later because if you don't you could lose everything."

"Thanks again, Di for coming over." Alyssa walked Diamond to the door and ponders on her next move.

Junior gave Diamond about fifteen minutes to get settled in when she returned to the office before he knocked on her door. He wondered why she went to see Alyssa so early this morning and why she or Alyssa didn't let him know they were meeting. He didn't like the strain the accident seemed to have cause between Diamond and Alyssa. He knew the only way to find out what really was going on was to ask his sister. He knew that she would look out for the best interest of all involved. After knocking on her door and her inviting him in, Junior sat across from Diamond ready to talk.

"Good morning, Di. Do you have a few minutes to talk?"

"Just a few, I need to get back into this new case."

"Okay, I'll get straight to the point. What's going on with Alyssa?"

"Why, are you asking me about your wife, Junior?"

"Because I know she is keeping something from me and since you are her attorney, I thought she may have been open with you."

"You know better than that, Junior. If I had a conversation with Alyssa as her attorney I wouldn't be able to discuss it with you."

"I understand all of that, Di, but I need to protect my family so if you know something please tell me."

"For the record, Junior, I'm no longer your wife's attorney?"

"So, you dropped her as a client this morning?"

"Wait a minute, why are you asking me that, Junior? I didn't tell you I communicated with Alyssa this morning."

"You didn't have to. I know you went to see Alyssa this morning."

"How, the hell to you know that, Junior?"

"Because I'm having Alyssa investigated. Dad is all over me about her. He feels Krystal's of all people instincts are right, that we shouldn't trust Alyssa."

"Well, this time big brother, I have to agree with Krystal. Something is going on with Alyssa. I declined to represent her this morning because I don't want to be privy to information I can't share with the family if I feel you guys should know."

"Di, she may be in trouble and we need to help her."

"I know there is trouble on the horizon and that is why I refused the case. Alyssa was anxious and scared this morning. I have never seen her when she wasn't confident so it was hard to turn her down because I wanted to help her."

"So where do we go from here, Di? I don't want Dad to get involved."

"I think we should give it a few days to let the investigators do their job. In the meantime, you should try to get Alyssa to come clean with you."

"Thanks, Di. I'll let you get back to work. I just want to keep my family out of harm's way." Junior left Diamond's office praying that he could get Alyssa to open up to him.

Chapter Sixteen

The sting operation couldn't have gone any worse. Alyssa sat and thought about how the agency set out to execute the plan that would end the case and let her go back to her family. Instead she was sitting in a dark room with her head hurting so bad it was hard to think straight. She left home this morning after kissing her daughter goodbye. She hoped that wouldn't be the last kiss she will give to her daughter.

Junior and Joe had already left for work and school, so she didn't have to make up a cover story to them as to where she was going. Now that the case was coming to a close she hoped she could be honest with her new family. She now wished she had taken Diamond's advice and told Junior what was going on, but for security purposes she couldn't talk about the case. She could have explained it to Diamond if she had agreed to stay on as her attorney. From the family perspective she understood Diamond's decision, but on a personal level she needed to share with someone in Junior's family what was going on.

Alyssa was experienced enough to know when she was being tailed and when she couldn't shake the tail she tried to call Junior so she could hear his voice. The next thing she remembered was being knocked off the road. She wondered what happened to her backup.

Calling to check in before the crash, the phone was knocked out of her hand before it could be answered. Now as the door slowly opened up, all she could do was sit in the chair she was tied up in and wondered which one of the subjects would be joining her. As the figure came furthered in to the room, Alyssa was face-to-face with the person she hated most in the world.

"Lyssa, Lyssa, Lyssa. Do you think you and that weak ass agency was going to get one over your mom." Amanda asked her daughter. "Don't feel like talking? How's the head?"

"Untie me right now, you old hag."

"Still disrespectful as ever. Hold on I owe you something." Amanda took her gloves off and smacked Alyssa so hard her ears were ringing. "Payback is a bitch isn't it, little girl?" Amanda asked.

"You need to turn yourself in while you have the chance." Alyssa said.

"I thought you were a smart girl. There is no way in hell I will turn myself in. You should have left the agency like you were supposed to instead of trying to bring me down."

"You are going down. You're like a mangy dog that needs to be put out of its misery."

"From where I'm standing you are the one that is going down. I knew when you were born you were too hateful for your own good. Why do you think I wanted to get rid of you?" Amanda started pacing the room. "The last straw was when you kept my granddaughter away and on top of that you had the nerve to put your hands on me." Amanda walked across the room and slapped Alyssa again. She was about to hit her again when there was a knock on the door. Amanda gave Alyssa a disgusted look and walked out the door.

Junior, Diamond, and two investigators from the firm sat outside of the abandon building waiting on the police to get there. They followed Alyssa when she left the house that morning. They knew something was going down today, because of the tap they put on Alyssa's phone. Junior didn't like that Alyssa was still working with Kane Karter. He was under the impression that she had ended her job with the FBI. When his investigator told him about this case Junior felt betrayed. He tried to convince Diamond not to come with them, but she insisted on being there.

One thing Junior was sure of is that he still loved Alyssa and will fight for their marriage. He knew that she loved him too. Junior had his mama issues, but he couldn't imagine what it was like for Alyssa for the first fourteen years of her life living with Amanda. The few details she told Junior about her time with Amanda didn't touch on the horror that was uncovered. Junior didn't get a chance to continue with his thoughts because of his vibrating cell phone. Recognizing the cell phone number of the investigator he had stationed at his house alarmed him.

"Is everything alright there?" Junior asked.

"It is now, but we had a situation that has been neutralized."

"What happen?" Junior asked a little louder than he wanted to.

"Well, a few minutes after your sisters arrived with the baby, a couple of thugs attempted to get into the house."

"Oh my God, is everyone okay?"

"Yes. The police have the two suspects in custody. It seemed they were told to snatch the baby."

"We can't leave until the police get here. As soon as they have things under control here we'll be right there. Tell my sisters to stay put. Don't let Krystal talk her way out of leaving." Junior ended the call.

"What happen, Junior?" Diamond asked

"Someone tried to snatch the baby. Dior and Krystal is at my house. I gave orders for them not to leave until we get there."

"This is bigger than we thought. They must be trying to break Alyssa down."

"That mom of hers is a piece of work. I'm so pissed that Alyssa would take this assignment and not let the family know of the danger."

"Junior, you can be pissed later. Right now we got to get to your house to see what is going on. Kane and three other agents are here to protect Alyssa."

"You're right, Di. Boys let's head to my house."

Chapter Seventeen

Junior sat in his family room surrounded by his family in shock. He couldn't believe what has happened over the last few hours since he returned home. Nick sat next to him on the loveseat. Joe and Annika were upstairs guarded by two police officers. The war between Alyssa and her mom had escalated to levels no one could have foreseen. The bottom line is Junior had to choose between his wife and daughter. Amanda told Junior the only way she would let Alyssa go is if they turn the baby over to her.

Most of the Morgan family was sympathetic with Junior's dilemma, but they had no intention of risking the baby's life. Twenty minutes after Junior and Diamond arrived at Junior's house the head of the FBI called Junior and told him about the gunfire. He explained they talked to Alyssa and that she was still alive, but was told if the baby wasn't delivered to them Alyssa would be delivered to him in pieces. It seemed Amanda in her crazy mind feels she can start over and be a good mom if she had the right baby. Now with less than four hours to go, Junior was beside himself.

"Dad, our guys are good, we can pull this off." Junior insisted.

"Son, you can't put your daughter in harm's way."

"I'm not, Dad. With the FBI, police, and our guys, I know we can find a way to make this work."

Kristina felt bad for her brother and had to fight with the rest of the family just to be there, but she had to help her brother. "Junior, no parent should have to be put in this positon. We can only imagine what you are going through, but Alyssa is a grown woman that can take care of herself, Nika can't."

"I know. I don't know what to do. I can't let my wife die. She needs me and I know she must be terrified." Junior said close to tears.

Diamond spoke up, "Junior, I'm not placing blame, but this situation could have been avoided if Alyssa was up front with us."

"Now, I bet you guys will listen to me. I told all of you that she was trouble." Krystal said with tears in her eyes.

"She was just doing this one last job for the agency. She didn't expect things to get out of hand. You have no room to criticize, Krystal." Junior said angrily.

"All of you stop it right now. Junior, we will stand by you one hundred percent, but you have to realize we can't use the baby that way." Bethany explained.

"I'm not talking about using Nika, I'm saying we could set up a decoy."

"Well, it seems the best we can do now is to wait until the FBI get here to see what they suggest." Nick said.

"Cool, let's talk about something else." Junior and his family made small talk while they waited for the FBI to arrive.

Alyssa still sat in the same chair she'd been sitting in for hours. She wondered what happened to Kane and the team. Why haven't they rescued her yet? She had a quick visit from Amanda where she told Alyssa she was going to see how much her husband loved her.

"What are you planning?"

"Don't start with all the questions, little girl."

"What are you planning on doing with me?"

"A bright girl like you should know the answer to that ridiculous question."

"You're not going to get away with this."

"Who's going to stop me?" Amanda asked.

"Just let me go and surrender. I will see that they be fair."

Amanda laughed so loud and hard she could have woke the dead, "I know you don't think I will be stupid enough to trust you to do right by me. You almost got me killed once before. I will never put myself in that position again." Amanda left the room as quickly as she entered it.

Now minutes later Alyssa had the bad feeling she wasn't going to make it out of this situation alive. She wished she had told Junior how much she loved him. With tears rolling down her swollen face she worried about her baby growing up without a mom and about how Joe wasn't going to have anyone to confide in now that she wasn't available. She knew it was wrong to keep Joe's problems away from Junior, but she had to make sure Joe felt he would confide in her.

Alyssa knew the Morgan family would help Junior to raise her baby, but she wanted to be there for her daughter. If something happened to her, she knew one Morgan that wouldn't shed a tear, Krystal. She still blamed Alyssa for the trouble she gotten herself into. If it was up to her, she would have made sure Krystal did jail time. This case was never ending. The bureau thought they had the head of the crime family until new information came in and when she saw the picture of Amanda she knew that she had to put her away once and for all. She asked Amanda if Krystal knew her and all Amanda would do was smile.

Cold water dumped on her head brought Alyssa out of her daydream. Seeing Amanda standing there smiling in front of her made Alyssa fighting mad. She couldn't wait until she got the chance to beat the shit out that heifer.

"Next time you will answer me when I'm talking to you."

"Are you planning on giving me something to eat and drink?" Alyssa asked.

"Nope, I'm not wasting my food and drink on you. I have good news and bad news, which would you like to hear first?"

"I want to hear that you have been taken out of your misery."

"The good news is it seems like your husband loves you. He has agreed to my demand. The bad news is that I'm not going to give him what he wants the most, you."

"What the hell are you talking about?"

"Well, it seems that your hubby isn't a good daddy."

"Look who's talking, the world's worst parent walking the earth."

"You know what he is planning on doing. He is going to sacrifice my granddaughter to save your sorry ass."

"I told you not to mention my, daughter."

"Why not, she is going to have a new mom soon."

Alyssa dreaded this was coming, but she thought her mom would at least spare her life.

"Junior would not put our daughter in harm's way." Alyssa insisted.

"If that was the case, why would he agree to hand her over to me in exchange for you?"

Alyssa was shocked. She hoped Amanda was talking out of the side of her head. There was no way Junior will hand their daughter over to this mad woman. "You're lying. Junior wouldn't trade our baby for anyone."

"For your sake, he better not be playing any games. I will raise that little girl to be just like me. Since I failed so miserably with you, I can have another shot at it with that sweet baby."

"You are going to regret the day you brought your ass back into my life."

"I already do. I just want my granddaughter then we will be done forever." Amanda left Alyssa to her thoughts after she made that statement.

Chapter Eighteen

Junior was glad when the FBI finally showed up. He didn't like the fact that Kane was with them, but his main concern was getting his wife back safely. They didn't have any good news to report. Kane explained that they (he and another agent) were staking out the warehouse Amanda was using as her meeting ground.

"When Alyssa arrived everything happened so quickly. Two guys in an old Chevy pick-up blocked Alyssa in and Amanda came up behind her once they took Alyssa out of her car and hit her over the head. They carried her into the warehouse afterwards."

"What the hell you two were doing while they attacked my wife?" Junior asked.

"We couldn't comprise the operation. If we had rushed in without backup, all of us would have been compromised." Kane explained.

"Look, my agents followed protocol. Agent Morgan knows the drill. She will survive this. She is a trained negotiator." The FBI leader said.

"This isn't a normal hostage situation. Alyssa's mom hates her. She did unspeakable things to Alyssa when she was a little girl." Junior said.

"We know her background. That is why we wanted her to take a backseat on this one. The main reason we came over was to talk to you Ms. Morgan. "The FBI leader said to Krystal.

"Hold on a minute. What do you want with my sister?" Diamond asked.

"She was part of the initial investigation years ago and may be able to help."

"Krystal will not be answering any of your questions at this time." Nick said getting up going over to sit by his youngest daughter.

"Dad if Krystal have information that could help save Alyssa, she needs to start talking." Junior said.

"Son, I know you're worried about your wife, but we have to protect out family." Nick said.

"Alyssa is part of this family too. She deserves to be protected." Junior persisted.

"She is a big bad FBI agent. I'm sure she will be okay." Krystal added.

"What the hell do you know, Krystal?" Junior asked his baby sister.

"I never met her. I just heard Ty and the others talking about her a few times." Krystal answered.

"What did they say about her, Krystal?" Kane asked.

"That she was not to be played with and anyone that turned against her was signing their death warrant. Since I like living I'm not going to say anything." Krystal rolled her eyes at Junior and folded her arms.

"Listen, you selfish brat, you're going to tell these people what they need to know." Junior said. Nick had to step in front of Junior to keep him away from Krystal.

"I don't know why you mad at me, Junior. Alyssa shouldn't have taken this case. She wanted to stick it to her mom so bad that she didn't think about putting all of us in danger." Krystal said not backing down.

"All I have to say is nothing better not happen to my wife." Junior left the room before he said or did something he couldn't take back.

The exchange was schedule to happen within the next fifteen minutes. Junior was the only family member part of the drop. Diamond was mad at her family, especially her Dad and Dillon because they didn't let her go. Junior explained there was no need for her to be there and the less people the authorities had to protect the better.

The FBI knew they had a small advantage because Amanda arranged the drop on the other side of town away from the warehouse. This made Junior nervous because the agents didn't think Amanda would take the change on Alyssa getting the drop on her. Moving her across town made that a possibility. The four people in the van were quite when they saw a dark vehicle approaching.

Going on the assumption the vehicle was a decoy; the men were on high alert. They didn't want Junior to do the exchange, but Amanda insisted. As the vehicle slowed down a few feet from the van they watched two armed men exit from the front driver and passenger side doors. Once they came around the car the back driver's side door opened and Alyssa tie, gagged, and blindfolded was pushed to the ground. Junior attempted to exit the van, but Kane wouldn't let him.

"Get your damn hands, off of me." Junior told Kane.

"You can't play her game, Junior. We are not going to let your emotions put all our lives in jeopardy." Kane said.

"Well, you guys better get off your asses and go save my wife."

They all looked on when Amanda came up behind a battered, bruised, and now standing Alyssa with a big knife at her throat. She remove the blindfold. The FBI leader said over the bullhorn.

"You have no way out. Let Agent Morgan go, Jones."

"Not until you give me my grandbaby." Amanda said, holding the knife closer to Alyssa throat.

"Are you ok, Morgan?" The FBI leader asked.

"I'm hanging in there, Sir." Alyssa responded.

"Cut out the damn chit chat. I want my grandbaby right now." Amanda demanded.

"No worries, you have to meet me halfway."

"That's not part of the agreement. Where is my son-in-law?"

"What difference does it make who hand off? I'm ready when you are."

"If I have to repeat myself one more time you will be picking my dear sweet daughter's head up off the ground."

"Okay, calm down. Mr. Morgan is right here. He will exit the van slowly." Nodding to Junior, to slowly leave the van Junior picked up the baby seat and took a few steps out.

Once he was in view Amanda said, "Turn the car seat around, Son. I want to make sure this isn't a trick." Amanda directed.

Junior slowly turned the car seat in the direction of Amanda and Alyssa. He prayed this would work.

A big smile spread across Amanda's face. "Oh my God, she is here." Amanda said and nodded for the two men to come over by her and Alyssa.

"Amanda, please don't do this. She is just a baby." Junior pleaded

"A baby that the two of you banish me from seeing, I just wanted to get a chance to know her." Amanda said softly.

Back in the van the FBI leader whispered into a small device that Junior had in his ear. "Keep her talking. The baby is the only link to keep her from going over the deep end. We have never seen this side of her, so we need to work it to our advantage.

"What if the three of us sit down and come up with a visitation schedule?" Junior asked.

Amanda voice turned evil again. "Boy, don't play me for a damn fool. That ship has sailed. I approached you guys several times to work out something. Too bad I'm not going be able to let you guys see my angel after tonight. She needs the love of a strong woman. Bringing her here to trade for my worthless daughter shows me you are not man enough to take care of my grandbaby." Amanda was pacing in a little circle near Alyssa and the two men.

"I didn't know enough about the situation. I'm sure once we get to know each other we can work something out….Junior stop in mid-sentence when Amanda went over to Alyssa and slashed her arm.

"Stop stalling. I'm not sharing her with the likes of you two. Now bring me my grandbaby or I will start cutting this one limb to limb." Amanda demanded.

Seeing that the situation was getting out of control the lead agent stepped in. "Calm down Jones. Junior walk over to hand over the baby." He felt Junior had brought them enough time to disarm the two guys that were holding Alyssa.

The next few minutes all hell broke loose. As Amanda walked towards Junior with the knife still in her hand she was tackled to the. The two men holding Alyssa were disarmed before they could take aim. Kane ran over to move Alyssa out of the way when all of the sudden Amanda broke free from the two agents that held her.

Junior still in shock was still standing in the same spot with the car seat in his hand. Amanda grabbed the car seat from Junior's hands and started to run in the direction behind the van. All of the sudden she stopped and looked down and noticed that she wasn't carrying a baby after all. Charging at Junior Amanda grabbed a smaller knife out of her pocket. Just as she launched at Junior the two agents she broke free from begin firing their weapons. As Amanda felled to the ground she was able to swing the knife and cut Junior across his stomach. All Junior remember was darkness as he fell to the ground.

Chapter Nineteen

At the hospital hours later the family sat in the emergency waiting room at the hospital to get an update on Junior's condition. Alyssa was also in the hospital, but outside of Diamond, Kristina, and their husbands the rest of the family didn't seem to care about how Alyssa was doing. As the girls and their husbands talked about the situation Diamond showed her frustration.

"I knew I should have been there. I may have been able to talk Amanda down so no one would have gotten hurt."

"Di, that woman was crazy as hell. You were not going to be able to talk her down." Dillon insisted.

"Well, I could have tried. We need to tie this case up. How are we supposed to do that with the head honcho dead?"

"We are not supposed to do anything. This is the FBI case not yours. I'm going to say it again, Krystal needs to come clean." Dillon persisted.

"Dillon, we can't blame this on Krystal. She has worked hard to turn her life around. Just because the FBI feels she knows more than what she is telling doesn't mean it is true." Kristina chimed in.

"Kristy, you know good and well Krystal is still hiding something. She is going to keep doing it as long as the family keeps babying her." Reggie said.

"Where is it going to get us to blame all of this on Krystal?" Kristina asked.

"We shouldn't worry about this right now. I think we should go back to check on Junior. The doctors said that was a nasty gash he taken." Dillon said.

"You and Di can go while Reg and I stay here. Somebody needs to be here to support Alyssa." Kristina suggested.

"Kristy, I know where you are going with this, but you can't blame the family for being upset. Alyssa should have let us know that the family was in possible danger." Diamond said.

"I know, I'm not condoning her actions, Di. I just know when Junior is feeling better he is going to want the family to support his marriage. We have to try to convince the others that Alyssa was misguided in her actions."

"I understand, Kristy. I like Alyssa and think she is good for our brother. We will go check on Junior and let you guys know how he is doing." Diamond and Dillion left Kristina and Reggie to stay with Alyssa while they joined the others waiting on an update on Junior.

Junior opened his eyes to a semi dark serene room. It felt like he was dreaming, but he knew he wasn't when his mind traveled to his last conscious memory of Amanda coming after him with a knife. Before he had time to react he heard the gunfire. That was his last thought, until he thought about his wife and tried to get up, but he wasn't able to sit up. Looking down at his arms in restraints, Junior wondered what the hell was going on and started moaning. Joe was by his side seconds later.

"Dad, you have to be still." Joe pushed the button to let the nurse know Junior was awake. She came into the room and asked Joe to wait outside until she checked his dad out. Joe went back to the waiting room where the other family members were waiting. They took turns visiting Junior once he was moved into a room after his surgery.

""My, Dad woke up, but the nurse sent me out of the room so she could check on him."

Nick and Bethany stood and gave Joe a hug. The rest of the family was relieved. Diamond volunteered to go see Alyssa and let her know Junior was awake. The doctor and nurse came out to talk to the family.

"Mr. Morgan had to be sedated. He will be out for the rest of the night. It is best you all go home and come back in the morning." The doctor said.

"Why did you have to sedate my, son?" Nick asked.

"The same reason we had to put him in restraints. We have to keep him from moving around too much so he won't tear his sutures open. He keeps asking for his, wife."

"My daughter is going to let her know Junior was awake. She is a patient here too at the moment. I'll let my daughter know Junior won't be up for visitors tonight."

"Mr. Morgan is going to be okay. I expect we will only have to keep him for a few days, barring any complications."

"Thank you, doctor." The doctor and nurse left while Nick joined the rest of the family.

"I had hoped the surgery would knock some sense into Junior." Krystal said.

"Krystal now is not the time." Kristina warned her baby sister. She and Reggie came to check on Junior once they knew Alyssa was okay.

"When will be the right time, Kristy? Our brother is on his death bed because of his sorry wife." Krystal persisted.

"Auntie, that is not fair. Alyssa has been good for my, dad. She is working hard to be a part of our family." Joe said.

"Cut it out, Krystal." Bethany said to her daughter.

"The doctor said Junior will be out for the rest of the night and that we should go home and come back tomorrow." Nick said once he was back with the family.

"You, guys can go home. Reg and I will wait here until Di and Dillon get back." Kristina said.

"Okay, Kristy. Make sure you guys don't stay too long. You need your rest." Bethany said.

All the family left except for Kristina and Reggie. They waited the half hour it took Diamond and Dillon to come back. Once they were updated on Junior's condition, they all headed for home.

Chapter Twenty

Junior been home from the hospital for only a few hours, but wished he was alone with his wife and kids. He loved his family very much, but sometime they could be overwhelming. Dior and Krystal had already left to go to the daycare, but Diamond and Dillon just arrived because she had to conduct the Monday morning meeting. His dad was still giving Alyssa the cold shoulder. This time he couldn't count on Bethany to calm his dad down because she felt the same way, but she wasn't as cold as his dad.

Kristina tried to make them understand that Alyssa realized her mistake and she was sorry for her cocky attitude thinking that she could take Amanda down without involving the family. Since both Junior and Alyssa were still recuperating they agreed to let Annika go home with Nick and Bethany. They were done with the packing and was about to leave when Alyssa asked if she could talk to Nick and Bethany alone. They left the room to go into Junior home office. Junior didn't know what his wife was planning, but hoped she knew what she was doing.

"I hope this goes as she expected. I don't think she will win those two over anytime soon." Junior said.

"She has to start somewhere. You know Dad will eventually come around, but with Mom not smoothing things over it going to take longer than usual." Diamond said.

"Junior, just be patient. I have to leave now, big brother. Call me if you need anything. I have two appointments this afternoon that I can't reschedule." Kristina said.

"Thanks, Kristy. Tell Reg, I said thanks for everything. We will have that men's night as soon as I feel stronger." Junior said.

"Not anything soon I hope." Diamond said.

"Why not, baby." Dillon asked.

"Because you guys take things too far and don't know when to come home on your nights out."

"Stop complaining, Di. We only have our downtime two-three times a year compared to you and the girls six-seven." Dillon said.

"I'm leaving on that note. Take care, you guys." Kristina gave everybody a hug and left.

"I hope she is getting enough rest. I think she should cut back on her schedule." Junior said.

"Don't try to shift gears, Junior. You know we need to talk about what happens next." Diamond said.

"What do you mean what happens next, Di." Junior asked innocently.

"Alyssa's debriefing is tomorrow. Is she resigning?"

"Di, I just got home. We haven't had the chance to talk about it." Junior explained.

"Well, we had a talk yesterday when I picked her up from the hospital. I think her job is in her blood. I don't know if she will be able to give it up, even if she truly wants to."

"After what happen I think you are wrong, Di. Anyway, she doesn't have to give it up completely. She could join our security team, do some work at the station, or open up a PI company." Junior suggested.

"Junior, I don't think you understand how that life can get into your blood. I know if I had to give up being an attorney, I would go stir crazy."

"Di, Alyssa made a choice to come here, married Junior, and be a step-mom to Joe. For the sake of her family she needs to realize if she stays in that line of work danger is always going to be a possibility." Dillon added.

"Well, in the end that is for her and Junior to decide. Junior, tell Mom and Dad we will see them later." Diamond went over to the recliner Junior was sitting in and gave him a slight hug. She didn't want him to move too much.

"Sure thing, Di, I know where you are coming from. Alyssa and I have important decisions to make." Junior watched his sister and brother-in-law leave the room and wondered how the conversation was going between his wife, dad, and step-mom.

The trio entered Junior's home office with grim looks on their faces. Alyssa knew she had a lot of making up to do with her new family. To be truthful she didn't care if Krystal never came around, but she knew she had to make things right with Nick and Bethany. When they were seated Alyssa started the conversation off by apologizing again for what seemed like the hundredth time.

"Mr. Nick, Ms Bethany, I know you guys are not happy with me right now. I had to finish this last case so there wouldn't be any future threats."

"I know you are not going to tell me if Amanda wasn't involved you wouldn't have gotten involved with this case." Nick said.

"She was part of the reason. Maybe a big part of why I wanted in, but the real reason was Krystal." Alyssa explained.

"What does our daughter have to do with your taking this dangerous assignment?" Bethany asked.

"I felt somewhere down the line if the operation wasn't completely shut down, the FBI wouldn't think twice about revisiting charging Krystal in the future." Alyssa thought before she continued, "To be totally honest if it wasn't for Diamond and Junior, I would have let things stand and not try to protect that selfish girl from herself."

"You need to watch how you talk about my daughter. I know what she held back was wrong, but she has worked hard to change her life." Nick warned.

"Mr. Nick, I don't want to be critical of Krystal, but I have come to care a great deal about your family. Even though she has changed she is still not beyond using you guys or anyone else to get what she wants."

"Again, this is not about Krystal. This is about the danger you brought to all of my family. No matter what, you should have stayed in New York if you had to work this case."

"I wouldn't have been able to draw Amanda out if I didn't move here and start my family. I know how she thinks and that she wouldn't be able to resist the opportunity to be a part of my daughter's life."

"The bottom line is, you almost got my son killed and you divided my family when we were just starting to feel normalcy." Nick went on like Alyssa hadn't explained herself.

"That's all I have to say. Mr. Nick, Ms. Bethany, I hope one day soon you realize how much I love all of you and accept me flaws and all." Alyssa left the office with tears rolling down her face.

Two Months Later

Junior couldn't believe how much had changed over the last few months. He was almost back to one hundred percent after his surgery. Joe was doing exceptionally well with his new therapist and had finally decided to go to Morehouse in the fall. He was still a little sad about the ending of his relationship with Brianna, but knew it was for the best. Joe had grown so much since his scare with fatherhood. His relationship with Kristina was closer than ever. He told her on more than one occasion how she saved his life.

The best thing to come out of Joe's relationship with Brianna was

that at the end of the school year she and her family were going to move to New York. Kendra signed her on while Krystal agreed to be her mentor. This shocked the family the most. Junior, Alyssa, Joe, Brenna, and her parents had a meeting last month to bring closure to their children situation. Brianna cried through most of the meeting and Junior felt helpless that he couldn't help his son more to deal with the situation. When it was brought up that Brianna wanted to get into acting and modeling that is when Junior said he would ask for Krystal and Kendra's help.

Junior was relieved a few mornings after her talk with his Dad and Bethany, Alyssa decided to retire from the FBI and become a stay at home mom. So far things were going well. At times she would help out at Dillon's center and Dior's daycare. She made sure to schedule around Krystal's time at each location. The relationship between Alyssa and Krystal was better and to Junior's surprise, Krystal came over one morning out of the blue to apologize to Alyssa and wanted to make amends once the family found out about Alyssa's childhood.

Nick and Bethany also accepted Alyssa in the family. They apologized to her for how they treated her stating they were just worried about the safety of the family. With so much free time on her hands Alyssa started spending more time with Bethany and was happy to have a strong mother figured in her life again. Things were going so well Junior and Alyssa were talking about having another baby soon so Annika would a playmate since Joe would be leaving home soon.

Diamond and Alyssa's relationship was back on track, Diamond even agreed to become her attorney again after Alyssa was debrief and resign from the FBI. Diamond also made Krystal thank Alyssa for taking the last dangerous care in part to protect her. They all couldn't believe someone as diabolical as Amanda was taken down because she wanted a relationship with her granddaughter. They had worked the case for years not able to get remotely close to her. Although, it hurt Alyssa, she knew what made her bio mom evil mind tick and spear headed the plan that almost cost her and Junior their lives.

Junior and Alyssa have had several double dates with his siblings and their husbands over the last few months. Seeing how happy his wife and son were at this moment made Junior realized that no matter what a family challenges may be if they create an unbreakable bond, there is nothing that will tear them apart. Sitting back he smiled and thought to himself, *"There is never a dull moment in the Morgan family.*